Malayali
Memorial

ADVANCE PRAISE FOR THE BOOK

'Unni R. is easily one of the front-ranking writers of short fiction in Malayalam today. His deep perception of the paradoxes of existence, his profound understanding of complex relationships, and the range and variety of his themes and narrative structures come through vividly in this selection so sensitively and skilfully translated by J. Devika. I have no doubt this is going to be a unique experience for the readers and a splendid addition to the wealth of Indian fiction in translation'—**K. Satchidanandan**

'More often than not, Unni's stories are sharp, well-aimed kicks that overturn and expose the dirty underbelly of that beast, Malayali Brahmanical patriarchal morality. The translations of his latest stories by J. Devika appear in this collection. Unni never fails to remind the Malayali elite that their celebrated homeland is tiny in the mind, a bit of a back of the beyond in matters of the heart. But he is also intensely aware of the rich legacies of this homeland that he shares with them—Kerala—and of the need to cast a discerning eye on these riches. This gaze, at once critical and loving, generates the extraordinary creative depth that marks his writing. His subtle stories that irk the mainstream Malayali man are not easy to translate. But J. Devika, who respects the aesthetic play that fiction demands and who is at home in both Malayalam and English, succeeds in recreating their magic in her translations'—**Sarah Joseph**

Malayali Memorial

and other stories

UNNI R.

Translated from the Malayalam by J. DEVIKA

VINTAGE

An imprint of Penguin Random House

VINTAGE

Vintage is an imprint of the Penguin Random House group of companies
whose addresses can be found at global.penguinrandomhouse.com

Published by Penguin Random House India Pvt. Ltd
4th Floor, Capital Tower 1, MG Road,
Gurugram 122 002, Haryana, India

Penguin
Random House
India

First published in Vintage by Penguin Random House India 2024

ISBN 9780670099702

Typeset in Sabon LT Std by Manipal Technologies Limited, Manipal
Printed at Thomson Press India Ltd, New Delhi

www.penguin.co.in

MIX
Paper | Supporting
responsible forestry
FSC® C010615

To Merry

Contents

CONTENTS

Girl

and

Boy

'Just an hour and a half from here,' he said. 'Super place!'

'Is it safe?' the boy asked.

'Sure! Better than a five-star hotel!' His tongue drew a wet line on his upper lip.

He then conjured up a picture of the place with his words: 'Very airy and nice. There's nice soft grass, plenty of it—better than a foam bed! And around it, lots of lush growth and tall thickets. Even God above wouldn't know you're there.'

'What about the snakes?'

'Eda, take this from me, if a cobra tries to bite a fellow bent on some dirty shooting, that cobra's going to fall dead.'

'Don't call it dirty shooting and all that.'

'Huh! You aren't going there with your legally wedded wife, are you? You're taking a girl from your class. This is what we call doing it on the sly—dirty

3

shooting! I'll tell you how to reach the place; write it down if you want.'

* * *

'I am not going anywhere,' she said.

'Edi, it's all right! There isn't a soul anywhere around there. It's safe,' he reassured her.

'What's wrong with sitting in a place where there are people around?'

'How can I then hug and kiss you?'

'Why can't you? I have no problem with you hugging and kissing me!'

'What if someone tells my parents?'

'Oh, really? Trouble if it reaches your family! You think there won't be trouble if it reaches my family?'

'Your family is far away, isn't it? In Wayanad.'

'Ah, right! People from Wayanad don't notice anything happening around them! They just don't comprehend anything!'

'Look, don't fuss, okay? I didn't mean that.'

She threw him a glance.

He touched her fingertips lightly and continued his pleading. 'Edi, let's go just once, please. I'll get you back to the hostel before six thirty, I promise!'

She swatted his hand off lightly and stayed quite still for a while, staring out of the window of the classroom.

'Let's do something—why not go to a movie?'

'What for?'

'You're the one so hungry for cuddles and kisses? You can do it in the dark there, in the movie theatre.'

'Ayyo, that's risky.'

She looked puzzled.

'The movie theatres are all fitted with security cameras. They work in the dark too. Will catch everything!'

She thought for a while and then said: 'In that case, let's postpone all this until after our wedding.'

That irritated him; he felt helpless and tearful. These feelings erupted in him together, and he almost fell at her feet.

'Someone will see,' she warned him.

'Let them!'

'This is what is called "obscene", Eda.'

Holding his shoulders, she made him stand up. He looked like he was going to burst into tears. Two teardrops massed in the corners of his eyes.

'Wipe your eyes,' she told him.

He wiped them off. She touched his hand. He smiled mildly. She didn't smile back, but kept her gaze on him. They were silent for some time, just a breath away from each other.

'So, we'll go there tomorrow, right?' he asked.

She nodded in agreement.

'Hey,' he said, 'Bring a scarf, all right?'

'What for?' she asked looking confused.

'There'll be a lot of wind and dust when you sit behind me on the bike; you don't want that. Just tie it around your head like these radical fellows. It's quite the trend!'

'I don't want to. The wind and dust are nothing. I travel on the pillion of my Chachan's Bullet from Wayanad to Pala!'

'But that's your Chachan—your dad . . . Actually . . .' He was hesitant, but the words just jumped out. 'What if someone saw us?'

She slapped his hand, pushing it away.

'Please . . .'

'Who are you so scared of?' her voice rose. He, who was about to fall at her feet again, straightened up instantly.

'. . . I . . . the family, of course, and then the local people . . .'

'Okay, so then, just wind up all this right now!' When she got up to leave with these words, the two teardrops mentioned earlier, along with a couple of companions, leapt on to his cheeks.

She saw them, but strode out of the classroom pretending not to notice. She went some way, but then stopped and ran back.

He was still old-style when it came to venting his sorrow—face down on the desk, letting the tears flow down to the ground. Actually, he was practising it then.

She tapped his shoulder. He did not raise his head.

'I don't think much of the proverb about milk and crying babies—or crying boyfriends.'

He tried to figure out what she meant by the statement, even as he stared into the little corridor of darkness between his eyes and the ground under the desk. He didn't grasp the meaning, but her reference to milk made him drool a bit. The thought of sucking her nipples made his drooped-down neck-vertebrae straighten up towards her face; rather like his member leaping to life. Careful not to let slip even a tiny indication of his inner drooling, he said, 'I want to suckle your breasts.'

That, she had not anticipated. She felt as though his statement had touched both her breasts, safely tamed inside a thirty-four-inch bra. Carefully barring the sensation from showing on her face, she spat out: 'Cchhi!' But it did not hit him on the face strongly enough.

'I want to!' he repeated.

'Lower your voice!' she snapped.

She looked at his face. When it seemed as though his ravenous gaze might tear out both her breasts and flee, she suggested, 'Get up, come, let us go.'

As they walked together, she asked him, 'Why are you trying to romance me? You are so scared of your folks and the neighbours?'

'Not fear,' he said. 'Just want to make sure people don't know right now . . . just that.'

'Will you dump me in the end and say that your folks won't let you marry a Nazrani woman?'

'Now, now, what's this?' He touched her hand. 'I'll make a vow on Lord Vishnu of Guruvayoor . . . that I'll marry this Christian girl!'

She laughed.

'So . . . then . . . tomorrow . . .' As he twisted and turned, not knowing how to tell her again, she completed what he could not say: 'You've to cover yourself with a scarf!'

He nodded. But noticing that the clouds of anger were beginning to gather again, he quickly built the traditional ridge to stop the storm waters: 'Please, this is needed now. Please, please understand. I am the only child of two bureaucrats . . . there is some tension . . . should I stoke it right now . . . that's why . . .'

'Ah, good thing both my parents are farmers. What would we have done if they were bureaucrats, right?'

He didn't really get what she said.

* * *

'Not bad, not bad at all,' she said, looking around.

He was busy scanning the area to make sure no one was around.

'No one's growing any crops around here,' she noted, looking at the fallow fields that rolled on and on as far as the eye could reach. 'Shall we buy some paddy land here after we marry and become farmers?'

He did not reply; he was trying to figure out how to get on a small patch of raised land overrun with wild growth in the middle of the fields.

'Will the gandakashala rice grow here?' she asked.

He was feeling relieved at not finding signs of frequent visits by outsiders—beer bottles, cigarette stubs, used condoms. Feeling tired, he stretched his limbs.

'You're not listening to me.' She sounded angry.

'What did you say?'

'Your mind is somewhere else.'

'Hey, no. I am just checking if there's someone around here.'

'What if there is? Will they eat us up?'

'Not that . . .'

'Then?'

'Nothing. Don't get so pissed off!'

'I am not pissed off. You wanted to come here; I came. You are still not comfortable. That's why I am asking you!'

'No, not that, our safety . . .'

'If you feel there's a safety problem, come then, let's leave right away.'

'I didn't say that.'

She pulled out a water bottle from her bag and took a sip. Then held it out to him. He refused it with a wave of his hand.

He had found the path into the wild patch by then. A rough path hewed by those who went in and out occasionally. The place looked like a head of hair parted in the middle.

'Shall we walk a bit?' she asked.

'Walk after riding the bike for so long? Let's sit somewhere.'

She pointed to the wooden bridge across the water channel that connected the raised land and the fields. 'Okay, then let's go sit there.'

'Let's go sit inside there,' he said.

'Why go inside? Isn't it really nice here?'

The same old trio of anger-tears-disappointment appeared on his face again. Since they were yet undecided about where they were to flow out through—eyes or tongue—there was a pause. In the end, the eyes restaged the old drama.

'Why are your eyes welling up?'

Not letting go of the old-style, he said, 'Nothing.'

'Tell me, boy!'

'You don't give a paisa for what I say, do you?'

'What bad stuff happened here, to count the paisa?'

'You're teasing me! For wanting to go and sit inside there.'

'Isn't it enough to sit here? Why are you so stubborn about going in there?'

'I want to hug and kiss you. It won't be okay here.'

'You can do it anywhere. Have I told you not to do it?'

'Not that . . .'

'Then what?'

'Would be better with some . . . more privacy . . .' he muttered.

That amused her. 'There's nothing but privacy around here! Hug me, Eda!'

He did not reply, just looked at her. Her eyes fell on a long scar on his neck.

'This scar looks nice on you.'

But he was silent, still. She came up close, hugged him and pressed her lips to the scar. Her tongue traced the minus sign, leaving behind a wet trail.

His breath bloomed in her ear like the rearing call of a trumpet.

'Don't tickle me, boy!' she said, shaking her head, getting it off her ear.

He held her hand and said, 'Let's go over there.'

'What for? Why not right here?'

He held her close. 'There, we can sit close together like two plants. See, here, there's the huge sky above and the big fields all around. They keep staring at us.'

She turned to him with a slight smile. 'You know very well that I'll fall for this kind of talk, right?'

He laughed.

When they rode the bike on the rough path through the dense foliage, she asked, 'Why can't we leave the bike there?'

'It's been with us, this chap. Let it see what we are up to.'

'But we aren't up to anything?'

'Sure, sure . . . but still?'

'Isn't it that you are scared that someone may see the bike and check inside?'

The conversation stopped like the breath of someone who was swiftly hung to death.

'Don't push it in too much,' she said, 'If you are allergic to the sky and the fields, I am allergic to vehicles. Keep it here. No one's going to see it from outside.'

He stopped the bike and got off. She hung her bag on the handle. They put the bike's keys in her bag.

They walked and came upon a nice, round bed of grass.

'Wow, this is good,' she said, smiling. 'Honeymoon style!'

'Why don't we celebrate our honeymoon here?'

'Ah, by that time, other fellows would have taken over this place and built flats on it, my dear!'

'Then let's not wait. Let's just have our honeymoon now!'

'Ayyada! Look at him. I knew well that this was what was niggling you!'

'Hey, no, don't talk nonsense.'

'Your eyes go straight for my cleavage if I don't watch out for a moment!'

'Now . . . but anyone would do that.'

'Not just mine! I've seen you look at many girls in our class—at their bums and tits and all, like a butcher staring at a fat goat!'

'Pardon me!'

'I'll pardon you. I don't know about those women, though.'

He sat on the grass. Green, from leaves of tender ages to rotting ones that lay scattered all around.

'Lie down on my lap, here. Let me love you a little.'

'Why lie on your lap for that? Isn't it enough to sit down here and just hug?'

'No, but you do it this way, don't you? The style?'

She looked deep into his eyes. The effort made by his lips, brows and other such servants of his expression to convey the urgency of that request looked funny to her, but she did not laugh.

'You want to put your hand inside my dress. It'll be easier if I lie on your lap. Excellent strategy!'

The many muscles on his face that served to make up his expression instantly recoiled and assumed their normal position. Another guy, Mortification, took their place.

'It was a strategy, am I right?'

He nodded, agreeing. She was seeing so weak a nod for the very first time.

She put her head on his shoulder and said, 'Hey, boy, I didn't fall for your muscles or your head of hair or beard. I made a mistake.'

He shook her off his shoulder and asked, 'Mistake? Why do you say that?'

'Eda, sometimes we are in a hurry and jump on the wrong bus, don't we? Without reading the destination board? If we want, we can always ring the bell and jump off. Or, we can just continue. I'd thought of ringing the bell sometime in between. Then I decided not to.'

'Why?'

'I was in, wasn't I? Have to get a chance to get out first, right?'

He felt a rush of love for her then. He pulled her into the strength of his arms and kissed her covered breasts.

'My chachan says that boys like you have Che Guevera's flamboyant garb and that wimpy, weepy mind of old Venu Nagavalli's characters in the movies!'

He didn't get that either, but in the spirit of that guerrilla operation in the wild, he let himself smile.

She too could turn to traditional styles, like him, once in a while. 'Tell me,' she asked, 'how much do you love me?'

His strength drained away at that unexpected thrust.

'No, not your usual dialogues—as much as your sweat, as much as the sky, etc., etc. Tell me, how much, really?'

He sensed that the usual response he'd picked up from the movies—of taking her face in both hands, raising it, locking his eyes with hers and delivering the standard lines—might be too much here. So he slowly pressed his face on to her shoulder and debated whether to present the much-used line from popular movies and magazines, or to draw on the poor man's refuge, the Bible. But before he could decide, she asked again, 'What? You have nothing to say?'

'If I tell you what I thought, you will tease me.'

'Never mind, shoot!'

'That line from the Bible, the one that says, "Even if you don't clothe yourself, you must clothe her . . .", will it do?'

'Ayyo? Need we go that far? Do you have the strength to lift all that up and carry it all the way? Just tell me one thing for now, simply, so that I can be sure. Or else, I'll start hating myself. We have to have respect for ourselves, after all. That's why I am asking you. Tell me, do you really like me? Or is it just my body that you like?'

He did not reply. It was completely quiet there except for the murmur of the breeze blowing through the foliage.

'Loving the body isn't such a bad thing. Just that I need to know. Isn't it important for me to know which side of the scales weigh more in your love?'

He stayed silent for some time and then asked. 'Do we have to spoil this precious time with such questions?'

'Eda, I told you, I just need to be sure. That I came here, that I sit here with you now, that we may copulate here—shouldn't I know if it is out of love or if it is just what you men keep talking of, a hook-up?'

His eyes seemed fixed on the insects creeping and running on the leaves. He got up. 'Let's leave,' he said.

'Yes. But tell me, can you not answer my question?'

Like the chorus appearing in one of Kavalam Narayana Panicker's plays, the old-style tears ran into his eyes again.

'You don't trust me?'

'Did I say that?' she asked.

'A little earlier, you asked me how much I love you. Have you ever tried analysing the word "trust"— *vishvaasam*?'

No, she shook her head, since, as a student of English literature, she did not need to parse Malayalam words and phrases or fix their broken joints.

'If you take away "shvaasam"—which means "breath"—from that word, it is nothing at all.' His voice firmed up with authority. 'I am that word, and you are the shvaasam in it.'

It was this ability of his, to transform himself into someone who could utter ripe and mellow words, that had stopped her each time she had tried to get off that bus.

'Such big words in the mouth of a twenty-one-year-old!' she said, smiling slightly.

He tried to hide the sheer effort of saying so much, and hurried her.

'Come here,' she called.

He was not listening.

'Eda, I said, come here.'

He could not ignore or refuse this command. Faster than a stone from a slingshot, he fell into her arms. Her lips pulled up his lips like a fish hook.

* * *

'And then what happened?' the bed-ridden Sumathi Amma urged her husband. 'Where did you see all this from?'

'Will tell you,' Vasudevan gestured to her to be patient till the murmur of hunger in his tummy subsided somewhat.

Sumathi opened her cataract-covered eyes as much as she could.

'I just crouched there in the bushes quietly.'

'Did they see?'

'How could they? I didn't even breathe and the leaves covered me well. Nobody could see me.'

'And?'

'And what? The boy and girl started doing all they could do to each other.'

'Clothed?' Sumathi Amma was still curious.

'They took all their clothes off and piled them up on the bike, right at the start.'

'Why did they do that?'

Vasudevan was irritated. 'Look here, if you want to know such things, go and ask them. This nosiness is a bit too much!'

'Father of my kids, don't be mad. What happened next?'

'That boy was all muscle. When he was sucking her nipples, she was telling him, don't do it like a calf suckling!'

'And the boy?'

'Ah! He was more and more like a calf!'

'Did she like it?'

'Did she? She was murmuring something, her eyes shut, like she was praying or something.'

'And after that?'

'That boy was the hurrying sort. He wanted to fuck. The girl was saying, this is the last day, let's not do it.'

'Last day of what?'

'Her period, of course.'

'And he listened?'

'No, the guy was in a hurry! He just opened her legs and went in.'

'Father of my kids, he's some fellow!'

'Oh, no way! The fool didn't last. Went up and down the swing just two times and then fell on the ground in a heap!'

'Why was that?'

'That's all he had. The poor child—not strong.'

Sumathi thought that was a fine way of putting it. She giggled loudly.

'The girl was a fine one, though. She giggled louder than you now and the poor chap just folded up.' Vasudevan lowered his voice and continued, 'Then, seeing his blood-stained weenie, she said, "Oh this looks like a newborn baby!"'

Sumathi Amma laughed again. But she suddenly stopped to ask: 'Did the boy laugh too?'

'No. How could he? The silly sod! He began to leap to his feet, but she pulled him down hard and climbed on him. He tried to shake her off, but she said, go only after we've loved some more.'

'And did they make love?'

'Who knows? Didn't that pork from yesterday start stirring in my tummy then?'

'Would they have?' Sumathi Amma's curiosity was getting the worse of her.

19

'That boy doesn't have it in him for that. He has a body like those wild wrestlers, that is all.'

* * *

'Let's go now,' he said. 'There's a *chuttuvilakku* worship in the temple today. I have to be home for it.'

'Let's stay some more. Weren't you the one who was desperate to come?'

'Get up! Someone may see us, and that'll be bad enough.'

'You weren't so scared all this while?'

'Listen to me.' He tore her arm off his body forcefully and got up.

She did not reply. Just lay there, looking up at the little circle of sky made by the tall heads of the shrubs reaching into each other. Just when the fun of lying naked in the grass staring at the sky at this age reached her lips as a smile, she heard his loud cry. Leaping up instantly, she ran to the bike. He was sobbing pathetically, leaning on the bike. The sight left her speechless for a moment. Then she went up close and gently put her hand on his shoulder.

'Don't cry,' she said.

He shook away her hand and began to wail.

* * *

'Is Vasu Chetan at home?' Jose called out to Sumathi Amma.

'Who?' She answered from her bed.

'Kuttan's amme, this is me, Jose. Vasu Chetan asked me to come.'

'He'll be back; just gone to take a dump.'

'How are you, Kuttan's amme?'

'Ente Jose-ae! Don't ask me the same thing each time you come! Didn't I tell you—it is my fate to be bedridden like this, with a bad leg.'

'Don't say such things, please. Can anyone say when the time will come for the good Lord to heal and bless?'

Sumathi Amma said nothing to that.

Seeing Vasudevan, Jose, who was sitting on the half-wall of the veranda, stood up. Vasudevan gestured to him to sit, and going in, indicated that he would be back soon.

Waking up Sumathi Amma, who seemed to have dozed off already, he said, 'Jose paid seven thousand for the two mobile phones. He could have given us some more.'

'Why did you steal their clothes also?' she asked, sleepily.

'Got all of it. Just for fun!'

* * *

The colour of the sky turned red and then black.

When he began to sob loudly again, she yelled at him, 'Stop that, NOW!' The sob exited his throat instantly.

'I am not clothed,' she snapped, 'Will you clothe me?' He had no reply.

Between the two of them, life-breath, in two different speeds, rose and fell.

The night covered her with its black garments. She set down the burden of her body on that dark raiment and turning to him said: 'I am leaving. Are you coming?'

Originally published as
'Pennum Cherukkanum' in 2020

End a

Story?

No,

No . . .

The young man was hanged to death. The sweeper who came to ready his narrow cell for the next prisoner found cobwebs on its ceiling and brushed them off with his broom. The spider was trapped; the sweeper killed it before it could climb down the wall. After his duty hours, he flung his broom into the heap of tools. A lizard that was creeping around nearby extracted from the broom a story that had got matted up in the broken cobwebs. The spider had woven into its web a story that the condemned young man had recounted aloud in his cell. But when the cobwebs were swept off, many moments in the story were also lost. The lizard shared the story that it had retrieved with its friends. They, in turn, shared it with many others. Once, a crow happened to hear the story that was being passed around. It retold the tale to its mate in its raucous voice. A man, who overheard it, translated it into human language. Because he lacked the speed of Ganesha, who transcribed Vyasa's words, many sub-stories and idioms of the first story were now lost. Because it was incomplete, and since the political climate was not favourable, he did not show it to anyone and merely stowed it away carefully. One day, the authorities searched his room and found the handwritten copy. He was arrested. On the night of his hanging, another spider wove into a cobweb the story that he related.

Originally published as 'Katha Theerkkaanaakumo? Illa, Illa' in 2020

December

Every morning, his umma would call him: wake up, my lazy little one, see the sun rising! But when her voice pushed the door open and entered his room, he would snuggle even more under the blanket. He would evade her, turning into a piece of the sky untouched by light. All the creatures around him—the neighbour's dog and the cat and the trees—would tease him—hey lazy little one! But each day, his mother, the breeze, the cat, the trees, and all else renewed their belief that he would indeed see the sun some day. So they waited to see the lazy little child leave his bed and get up with the sleep still lingering in his eyes. But the little one tricked them all. He always stayed under the warm sheets and went on snoring.

One day, the lazy child woke up before his umma and the cat and the trees and all else, brushed the dark off his body, and got up. He opened the door soundlessly. The sun will now come up to see me from beyond the eastern horizon, he thought happily. He stood in the cool air that wrapped itself around his naked little body. He got goosebumps waiting for the sun to touch him! But as his eyes sped through the mist towards the far distance to catch a glimpse of the sun before it rose up in the sky, a terrible sound shook his tender ears. Used only to gentle childish noises, he was frightened. The blasts terrified him; they rang again and again; he wailed loudly. The house awoke rudely on hearing his wails. Umma ran up and seeing him stand there petrified, his eyes filled with fear, she hugged him close. He asked her, 'Umma, did I wake up late? Or is this the time of my awakening?'

Umma was silent. She stood there, staring wordlessly at the rising darkness.

Originally published as 'December' in 2020

Three
Love
Stories

And thus, from that moment—to be exact, at twenty-three seconds past ten—they ceased to be lovers. In the very next second, they had to enter a past in which they had been lovers. That left both of them slightly surprised—that the next second was not the future; that a past awaited them in the future. They did not wait to speak or remember their past. Because she had to get out of his narrow studio apartment quickly, she did not offer a gentle smile and an affirmation of any sort—that they would meet again, or that their lives would end without such a meeting. There was never too much talk between them. So even the glance that she threw at him before she stepped out was excessive.

It was when she walked away briskly through the hustle and bustle of the city that she noticed that her body felt extraordinarily light. It was then that she remembered that she had vomited in his room. She reversed her steps and ran back.

He opened the door only after she knocked repeatedly. He had been asleep, she noticed. She took a quick look around the room. She searched under the bed and the table, in the kitchen and bathroom. It was missing. He sat there watching her, his eyes clouded with the fatigue of daytime sleep.

She said, 'When I vomited yesterday, my heart fell somewhere here.'

'There was nothing to eat, so I ate it,' he told her.

'What to do now?' she asked.

'When I shit . . .'

The thought of her heart emerging out of his anus disgusted her.

She walked fast through the hubbub of the city, wondering if people, especially the young, noticed the void in her.

He, at that moment, was sitting on the toilet and straining to see if he could expel a heart that was too deep within him, too deep to be ever expelled.

* * *

The poet Changampuzha Krishna Pillai's famous pastoral elegy *Ramanan* laments the death of the penniless goatherd Ramanan, who, unable to bear his beloved's betrayal, the beauteous aristocrat called Chandrika, commits suicide. Nothing has been written since about what happened to his goats after his death. And therefore, the sub-inspector (SI) who had just taken charge took an interest in the matter. Though the more experienced policemen thought it was a bit like the overenthusiastic new bride sweeping the roof of her husband's home, nobody made an open objection.

They too went around in search of the goat. They found a flute where the goat once dwelt. That was evidence indeed. They went back to the police station, taking it with them. But to this SI, this was really nothing. He renewed the investigation. In the middle of it, he felt the need to scrutinize the matter more scientifically. The scientific investigator in him kept telling him that wherever they may be, Ramanan's goats were likely to show up at the music of his flute. That's how he decided to learn how to play the flute.

When night fell, the SI would step out of his khaki uniform and become a flute player. He would go to the backyard of each and every house there and play the flute. Once, when he was doing this, a goat came out of a house and told him, 'I am Ramanan's goat. You must let me live.'

The SI was puzzled.

'We are together now.'

The SI saw Chandrika standing in the dim light beside the house.

'Ah, who's?' He was really uneasy.

'You should not see us through a policeman's eyes. Aren't you an artiste?'

The SI suddenly felt a rush of pride that he was an artiste too.

'But still . . .?' That was an artiste's skepticism.

'You are indeed an artiste,' the goat reminded him again.

As he turned to leave, the SI wondered whether it was a buck or a nanny goat. Do not think like an SI, the artiste in him chided.

The next day, the police traced Ramanan's goat to Chandrika's house. Now it lived in the police station, eating the jackfruit leaves that the policemen fed it. The SI fell into an unbearable dilemma.

This dilemma was related to the repeated surfacing in him of the question: Why the goat could not be left to living its own life? He escaped many a time telling himself that he was merely performing his duty as a police officer. But immediately, there would be the further question: Okay, so you are happy with doing that, but what about them? These questions were raised by the artiste in him who emerged when he took off his khaki uniform and picked up the flute. And soon, sick and tired of arguing endlessly and failing to receive a satisfying response from the SI, the poor artiste tucked the flute into his waistband and hung himself to death.

When he was preparing the FIR, the SI did not once look at him, or at his flute. But if by chance his eyes did fall on it, he prayed: Let the flute look like a lathi with holes drilled in it.

* * *

They decided to exchange underclothes for a whole day.

Before long it felt to her like a loose and hanging cup made of areca-frond tightened rather forcibly around the waist.

He too felt that it was a tight breathlessness pressing hard, almost biting the skin, down below.

They bore it till the evening like people used to keeping their word.

In the end, at night, they returned each other's undergarments.

They were washed and dried and the next morning, they wore those very underclothes. Somehow, somewhere, there was a lack of fit, a loosening, an unfamiliar . . .

Originally published as
'Moonnu Premakathakal' in 2020

Walking

The feet feel lethargic. Falling into lethargy while sitting down is not like feeling fatigued from walking. A newborn babe's feet are envious of its already-deft hands—that is pretty evident from the way its legs thrash about as it wails. The conceit of legs becomes apparent in that they doggedly pursue walking despite falling down a thousand times. The glimmer of power is clearly visible in the way we say that it is important to learn to stand on one's 'two feet'. And now? It has become impossible to take a single step beyond all these prohibiting lines, these *Lakshmanarekhas*. These feet that once walked briskly, ran swiftly, they are now trapped in the house, the room; they can't breathe. Some feet can't even remember: once, I used to walk. Some feet say: I have forgotten how to walk. There is no ennui worse than ours, complain other feet. Though far more unsoiled compared to earlier days, all feet protest against this state in which one is reduced to a dog who is not allowed to bark. They all grumble: when will we make our way through this whole world of helplessness and step beyond it?

If anyone does hear the plaints of certain feet that have not known a day or place of rest, that are covered with soil and mud, which ask, 'When will this trudge end?', 'When will these cracked and broken soles heal?', are we to believe that they are simply of people who don't pay enough attention to the care of their feet? In any case, why should one keep track of these plaints at all?

Originally published as 'Walking' in 2020

Sound

No one visited that library. Still, the librarian opened it every evening in the hope that someone might come to borrow a book. He would sit on the half-wall of the veranda of that old building for a short while. Then, getting up, he would go inside and sit on the chair—it was in worse shape than him—behind the table and start reading. Since the past few years, he had been reading the massive and authoritative dictionary, the *Sabdataaraavali*, by Srikanteswaram. Once the day's reading was over, he would replace it among the books in the reference section. He would then press down with his frail finger that inverted half-circle of iron that seemed reluctant to fall into the little well of the lock. Making sure that the lock wasn't hurt, he would check if it had actually clicked. By the time night fell, the librarian would have closed all the doors of the library and left.

It was on one such day when the librarian was replacing the *Sabdataaraavali* that he fell into it and was trapped inside. He tried to call out a couple of times. But he couldn't. He tried to shake himself free to run to safety, but his limbs were entangled in the words. He wanted to clap his hands and make a noise, but they were fixed firmly between two pages. His hands opened only when the pages opened. When he did not return home even after midnight, his wife and children went out looking for him. They came to the library. The librarian tried to call out to them to tell them that he was inside the dictionary, but he could not. He realized that though the title of the dictionary included the word 'sound'—*sabdam*—he could actually make no sound. His wife and children searched for him everywhere— under the almirahs and inside the drawer of the table even. They did not find him. The older son closed the door of the almirah containing reference books before they left. He locked it. The door of the library too. The family and the local community started searching for the missing librarian. They advertised in the newspapers. Complained to the police.

From the next day, naturally, the librarian stopped opening the library. One day, a thief who was trying to hide from the police sneaked in there. If only he could see me, the librarian wished fervently. But he did not. The thief would stay inside the library the whole day and go out at night When he got bored of waiting for the evening, the thief started browsing through the books.

The librarian saw this from inside the dictionary and was delighted. The sight of the very first reader in the library made his eyes well up with joy. But the thief just browsed, never read. But his hand reached every book. He touched the books. Let the books feel the joy of at least being touched by someone, prayed the librarian. But when the afternoons grew warmer, the thief would fan himself using the books. This was unbearable to the librarian. Unable to scold him or even make a noise, he sat quietly inside the *Sabdataaraavali*.

One day, the thief used a small iron wire and poked at the lock of the reference books almirah. Its doors fell apart, like two arms opening wide to the thief. He gawked at the books inside in the same way some people do when they see obese persons. He opened those big books one by one. *Some of them are heavier than they look*, he noted with surprise. Also, besides examining their weight, out of habit, he could not help checking whether there was something inside each. The disappointment of finding nothing inside even a single book was not befitting of his profession; he did not feel it. He took out each book one by one and opened them. *Sabdataaraavali* was placed next to *Amarakosam*.

When the thief pulled out *Amarakosam* and began to flip through it, the librarian's heart began to race. His hands are going to reach out to me next! He will see me when he flips through the pages, he thought. He will be startled, scared. Maybe he will scream. Or grab another book and swat me hard, killing me. He stayed there, eyes shut; not knowing what was going to happen when the thief pulled out the dictionary. Sensing it, a huge shiver came over him, covering him fully like a blanket. The book felt heavier than the others, so the thief carried it to the table with both hands. Then, as he turned the pages, he found a man, the fear taut on his face, scrunched between the pages. The sight of the fearful old man made him laugh. The librarian laughed too. Then, at that very moment, they heard the sound of someone knocking at the door. The thief believed that it was the police; the librarian was sure that it was the reader he had so long waited for.

Originally published as 'Sabdam' in 2020

Itinerant
in the
Mahabharata

[The Mahabharatham, it is believed, can cause domestic discord if kept and read in families. It ends, of course, with the Pandavas leaving everything behind, including family and society.]

'Tell me the truth.'
Chandran nodded.

'Did you engage in sexual activity together?'

Chandran was amazed when that high-Malayalam sentence, framed in perfect, formal language, came out of Maathukkutty's mouth. He looked dead serious. No, Chandran shook his head in the negative.

'Any kind of physical intimacy?'

'No.' Chandran nodded again.

Maathukutty's face fell. A sliver of disappointment played on it.

'Not even a kiss?'

'No.'

Hope died on Maathukutty's face and descended into oblivion. After much effort he climbed back, with a bottle of rum.

After three pegs, Chandran started to weep. When he began to sag from all that crying, a fourth peg was offered as support. He downed a mouthful of it and said, in a lilt that came from the tears loosening up the voice: 'A romance of ten whole years.'

Maathukutty's score on this matter, counting all the romances that had merely budded, died in the bud, or been plucked as a bloom, amounted to the first digit of ten. It was for him, therefore, like the coin in a pauper's pocket. But he pretended otherwise.

'How sad. How regrettable!'

Such formal utterances, not usual with Maathukutty, comforted Chandran. Someone speaking in a mature sort of way in a crisis, that is all one needs—a minor relief. Maathukutty was offering it with remarkable generosity. When it appeared that Chandran was beginning to sink within, like the liquor-level sinking down towards the floor of the bottle, Maathukutty tried to console him: 'This is life. Life is only this.'

'But still, how could she?' Chandran laid his head on the table. 'She was my life.'

'She fell in love with someone else. She left. Don't blame her.'

While going home, Maathukutty held Chandran with one hand and his bag in the other.

'The bag is heavy,' Maathukutty observed. 'What's in it? A piece of rock?'

'It is her last gift to me,' said Chandran. And he pressed his face on Maathukutty's shoulder and let loose a flood of tears. Maathukutty was not shaken. What if I say that this heavy thing seems to be her heart, he thought in the rum-induced high. But that was momentary. When he opened his mouth, it struck him as an extraordinarily cheesy thing to say, unfit for the mouth of someone as exalted as him.

'Chandra,' he asked. 'Did you take a look at the present?'

'No,' he said. 'Why don't you open the bag and look.'

'No, that won't be right,' Maathukutty replied. 'Isn't it something she gave you . . . when you were intimate? You alone should see it first.'

Chandran wanted to kiss Maathukutty then. Not able to do it, he collapsed, exhausted, on his shoulder, like a helpless baby.

* * *

Amma and Acchan looked puzzled. His pengal—sister, that is—alone got a sense that something was wrong.

She mentioned it privately to Amma: 'Maybe he got told off by a lover or something?'

'Go away,' Amma snapped at her angrily.

'Otherwise, why is he cooped up in his room, neither eating nor sleeping?'

Amma now groped at the reference to the lack of interest in food and sleep. This chap who couldn't bear a moment's hunger, and who could sleep anytime and for any length of time, if he was sitting all hunched up and moody, then something must be wrong.

'Edi,' she asked, 'is it some love affair gone wrong?'

'I have no clue! *Ariyaammela*!'

'Oh, *pinne*! Wasn't it you who suggested that?'

'I was just saying what I thought.'

Amma thought about it. Maybe better to ask directly. She went towards Chandran's room.

'Amme, are you going to ask him?'

'Yes.'

'Amme, please, if you fling it at him, he might do something drastic—try to kill himself or . . .'

'Stop saying horrible things,' said Amma, seizing the fallen stem of the coconut-palm frond and hurling it at her. She moved away quickly, but it hit her bum, and she let out a low scream.

At the moment when his sister's scream rose up and flew into Chandran's room, his lips were slowly slipping and falling from chanting to a sob.

Why do you cry, who harmed thee, child?
What transpired here, asked he who heard it.
'There, he's weeping,' his pengal said.

Amma, too, heard him cry. They ran up and knocked at his door. Chandran tried to control his sobs but they did not obey him; they continued to pace up and down the room noisily for some more time.

When they subsided, he opened the door. At that very moment, Amma let out a wail. Though he tried to console her, she insisted on knowing what was wrong with him.

'Nothing,' he assured her. 'I was just feeling sad about the future.' He vowed that nothing else was bothering him.

Amma told Pengal firmly that Chandran's father was not to know anything of his tears and words. She promised to be quiet. But Amma herself ended up telling her older brother the whole thing.

'Cried thinking of the future?' he asked.

'He cried. We both heard him.'

Her brother was silent for some time. 'He's a good student, isn't he?'

'Yes, he is.'

'Then why does he need to cry?' He was puzzled. 'Did he cry for his future or for the future of the country?'

'I know nothing about that, Chetta,' she said. 'Can you please ask him?'

He looked a bit doubtful about that too. 'If I come and ask him, his father may not like it.'

'Oh, he won't know. Better that you ask him. His father may give him a beating.'

Amma's brother came home the next morning after Chandran's father had gone to work.

'Where is he?'

'Still cooped up in his room.'

He hummed and went across to knock.

Chandran opened the door.

'Can I talk with you for a bit?'

He did not reply.

Amma was irritated. 'Didn't you hear your uncle?' she asked sharply.

Chandran nodded.

'Chetta, you just ask him,' she said, withdrawing.

Uncle stepped into Chandran's room. They spoke for some time and then Uncle came out of the room bidding him goodbye. Chandran closed the door again.

Amma hurried after her brother. He looked like he had uncovered the mystery.

'I've found out!'

Amma looked at his face expectantly.

'First, that thing must be removed.'

'What?'

'If it stays there, not just his, even my future will be lost.'

Feeling terrible that the future of her eighty-year-old brother would be a bleak one, Amma asked again: 'Please tell me what the matter is. Please put it straight.'

'Edi, things that should not be kept at home should not be allowed in. Our elders have always pointed that out! If you aren't careful, not just your family but the rest of us too will have to suffer!' Uncle went away with these words.

'Will be worse if we tell this to Acchan,' said Pengal. 'Amma, you should just go and speak to him.'

'Edi, he just can't understand some things,' replied Amma, 'Isn't he an innocent first-born kid?'

'In that case we'll have to tell Acchan.'

'Yes, and he'll burn down everything in that room.'

'Isn't it better to burn all of his things rather than allow that thing to remain there?'

'Yes, you're right,' agreed Amma. 'Why don't you come with me? Just to make me feel brave.'

'If I come, will it be like what Uncle said—a proper family feud?'

Chandran just looked straight into their faces and spoke a single line: 'For you, this may be just a book. For me, it is my whole life.'

Pengal wanted to say 'Shame!', but she resisted the impulse.

'Could be,' said Amma, gritting her teeth in sheer vexation, 'but don't mess up other people's lives also with this.'

'I want to be left in peace,' said Chandran, looking up at the ceiling.

'Eda Chetta,' Pengal said. 'You'd better take this away. Or I am going to tell Acchan. Your whole life will turn upside down if I do.'

They left the room. The fear they had left behind did not stay idle; it began to pace around him. When he was convinced about the danger of staying there under the circumstances, Chandran jumped up.

Maathukutty was so surprised, he looked like he was caught in a trap-net laid by surprise. He stared at Chandran. All he felt like telling him was, 'My dear Chandra, in truth, this must be the first time in all of history that a girl in a love relationship gave the guy such a parting gift!' But he was not able to say it and seemed frozen in that sitting pose.

'Maathukkutty,' Chandran called out. 'Tell me how to resolve this.'

He did not know. If it were a shirt or perfume or sweets, they could have just flung it into the Meenachil River, spat hard on the ground and walked away. That was impossible with this gift. If they cursed it and those words turned out a bit misshapen, it would be seen as intolerance or obscenity or . . . What was to be done now? Maathukkutty thought hard while they walked. Lost in thought, they reached Maathukkutty's room.

'Here, you can leave it here,' said Maathukkutty, opening an almirah.

Liquor bottles, half-finished, empty ones, condoms, underpants of many colours . . .

'But, my dear Maathukkutty, this is my . . .'

Maathukkutty interrupted Chandran instantly. 'I know what you are going to say. Eda, this is the safest place. You can put it anywhere inside here, wherever you please.'

Wiping off the cigarette ash and removing the cigarette butts and the ashtray, Chandran lowered his lover's parting gift on to the shelf.

'No one's going to take it from here,' Maathukkutty assured him.

'It's not enough to just keep it here. I need to read it every day.'

'Oh, cool. Come every day, whenever you want to, and read it.'

Before he left, Chandran made a request: 'Don't tear any pages from . . .'

'Cche!' Maathukkutty protested. 'Why should I do that? Isn't it why I am getting the English newspaper?'

Chandran nodded, as if to agree. Suddenly the man of sexual experiment leapt out from inside Maathukkutty. 'Hey, have you ever masturbated thinking of her?'

'My dear Maathukkutty, please don't ask me such things,' Chandran replied.

'Chandra,' Maathukutty began again, adding a drop of maturity to his voice, and pushing it towards him. 'Masturbation is no crime. And especially when you do it thinking of your girlfriend.'

'I can't do that, Maathukkutty.'

Maathukutty did not know what to say. In the end he asked, 'Have you done it with anyone at all in your mind?'

No, Chandran nodded. Why, Maathukkutty wanted to ask, but he decided against it when that sentence took birth in Chandran's choked voice: 'It is a vice—*adharmam*!'

* * *

Chandran's mother did not know where he went every single morning. Maathukkutty's Ammachi too could not make out what he was up to all day locked up in Maathukkutty's room. He wouldn't come out when it was time for lunch—just happy with a cup of black coffee sometime during the day.

One day, Maathukkutty's Ammachi met Chandran's Amma at the ration shop.

When she returned home, Ammachi told Mathukkutty, 'You bastard, you scoundrel, there's no trouble your old man and you haven't brought upon me. And now you've added a new member to your trouble-maker gang?'

Maathukkutty was taken aback. His uncle's daughter had been visiting them since the past week. Did Chandran transgress *dharma* and make a move?

'My Ammachi, Chandran is a good person. He's truthful. Won't cheat. It's okay to have him in the house!'

'You do that! But that book he's been reading, don't let it anywhere in here!'

'Aren't we true Christians, Ammachi?' Mathukkutty tried to reason. 'Should we be a bit . . .'

That half-framed sentence was shattered by a massive expletive that sprang out of Ammachi's mouth.

'I knew it! That some Satan had got in here when your older sister came here yesterday and kicked up all that fuss!'

When the voices began to rise thus outside, Chandran's eyes were wandering among the little sprouts of meaning that the letters created together on the page . . .

What do we do now? Maathukkutty and Chandran put their heads together. Actually, only Maathukkutty was really present. Chandran's mind was elsewhere.

'What if we do this?' Maathukkutty asked. Chandran looked at him.

'No one's going to let it into their houses anywhere around here,' he said. 'Why don't we take it to Velachi the curry-man? To keep it in his toddy shop?'

'To put it in a toddy shop?'

'My Chandra, the knife with which Pappachan was stabbed . . . it was in Velachi's shop for eight whole years. Did anyone find out?'

'Is this like that?'

'Eda, this isn't very different from getting stabbed. She was giving you a sharp blow, wasn't she? If you look closer, you might find more of your blood than the blood from all the fighting and war . . .'

Chandran literally waxed into fullness, like his namesake, the very full moon, in front of Maathukkutty's very eyes.

'I was just trying to see if you'd fall for a sentimental line!' Maathukkutty laughed.

* * *

Curry-man Velachi removed the paper covering the book, opened it, read a few lines, then drawing back sharply as though burned by a sudden bolt of lightning, said: 'No way!'

'Why, Velachi?' Maathukkutty asked.

'Edaa cherukkaa! This is a toddy shop. Not a puja room!'

'Leave it here. When I'm here to tipple, he'll come with me to read.'

'Go away, you skunk! Might as well set up a mic and start chanting prayers!'

'My Velachi, didn't I bring it here because I couldn't keep it at home?'

'Why? Is it porn or something?'

'No, but they say that if we keep it at home, there'll be feuds in the family!'

'Eda, Maathukkutty, isn't the toddy shop like a home? The drinkers here are one big family. Don't try to break it up. Go now, go.'

Maathukkutty looked at the image of Srinarayana Guru put up on the planks of the wooden wall of the shop. He was about to ask if it was indeed the Ideal Place where all lived like brothers beyond the divides of caste and religious hatred, when Chandran said, 'Let's go.'

'What to do now?' Maathukkutty asked.

Chandran did not say anything; he merely watched the sun come down.

'Say something!'

The darkness spread between them.

After some time Chandran recited a couplet:

All that are born are sure to die
At this we need not sigh

Chandran's soft chanting did not penetrate Maathukkutty's ears. Even though he asked a couple of times what Chandran meant by that, he did not reply. All Maathukkutty knew was that as the dark grew denser each minute, the two of them were sitting steeped in it on either side of a single breath.

'I'll sit here for some more time,' Chandran shook the sheet of dark slightly with his low voice. Sensing his meaning, Maathukkutty got up. He did not bid him goodbye. He lit a match and walked off in its light.

As it grew later and darker, Chandran got up. He walked past the Raveeshawaram paddy fields, past the Vattakkotta, and the rubber garden of the Peedika family. As he walked, Chandran heard muffled footsteps behind him. He did not turn around.

Kochu Mappila of Idappally, who had woken up for a leak, saw someone walking in the lane in front of his yard. He hurried to the side of the lane to see who it was, but the person had almost disappeared, and was just a vague shadow far ahead. As he watched the figure grow dim and disappear, he saw a dog follow him, calmly.

Originally published as
'Bharathaparyatanam' in 2018

Malayali
Memorial

This happened when S. Santhosh Nair was eight years old. I shouldn't really refer to it so lightly as 'this', so let me call it an incident, or even better, an event. It was yesterday that the gentleman in question came to see me. I refer to him as 'gentleman' because I do not find it improper to extend full respect to someone who will turn eighteen this December, who has completed his twelfth standard and is now in his first year at college in the degree course. Taking these into consideration, this is most dignified description that can be offered of Santhosh Nair.

I am just an ordinary person—no social activism, no poking my nose in politics. I get up every morning at four, go for my walk, sweep our front yard, help my wife in the kitchen and leave for work with her at exactly eight-thirty. In the evening, I watch the news for a bit, take a look at the children's homework and go to bed after an early dinner. Once in a while my wife and I have a beer together, without anyone, even the kids, knowing. She complains that my talk gets too spicy then! And not only that, on such nights, I insist on some particular styles in sex, but usually fall asleep in the middle of it.

In this whole life, the story of which can be condensed into this short paragraph, the only complaint about me that my family and friends have is regarding my inability to look at other people's faces directly. Much before we got married, my wife had scolded me about the way I walked, face down, looking at the ground. But though my face was thus averted, not a single passer-by could escape the glances that darted up from my eyes. That is how my eyes—these eyes that belong to the father of two young girls—began to anxiously follow Santhosh Nair and his friends who play badminton regularly near the library, then walk to the wayside eatery at Panambalam for a dosa, hang around chatting at the temple grounds and finally split up to go home.

My wife does not share this worry at all. She's proud of being the mother of two girls—that's all. No anxieties on that count bother her. They too are like their mother— they don't worry a bit about sitting with one leg crossed over the other, about whistling loudly at dusk or about going all over town on their bicycles. Sometimes they bring their washed bras and panties, and ask me to hang them on the clothesline to dry!

Though it is like this in our house, it is out of the boredom of being a simple father that I began to memorize the comings and goings of some young men near our girls' ages or a few years older than them. When we sit down to supper, I always try to make a comment or two about them, but because the girls are quite adept at anticipating my moves, my comments never gain even a single inch. And thus many, many of my opinions and observations are dashed to death in the embryonic stage itself. It is one of these young men, Santhosh Nair, who, quite unexpectedly, paid me a visit.

I had just got back from office, washed my face and feet and was about to plant a hibiscus branch that I had plucked on my way back when I heard the rusty gate open and saw Santhosh Nair enter the yard briskly. I first looked at his hands, and then at the pockets of his pants and shirt. I saw nothing unnatural. But because my heart was pounding so hard, I found it difficult to get up from where I was squatting. He was quite close to me by then, and must have surely heard my heartbeat hard. He, however, paid no attention to it and asked me in the same quick-paced manner: 'Chetta, I have something to tell you.'

The hibiscus branch that I held inserted itself into the soil without even asking my permission. When I continued to sit there without attempting to brush off the dirt on my fingers on my mundu or pull my gaze off the ground, he repeated: 'I have something to tell you.'

I nodded, summoning a bit of courage from somewhere, but was unable to move at all from where I was squatting.

'It's not something I can tell you here.'

This made me stand up at once. I could hear the chatter of my wife and girls from inside the house. No one had noticed this visitor. Because I did not know his intentions, I asked him, quite hesitantly, 'Isn't it enough to talk here?'

'No,' he replied, and his voice seemed to brim with a certain arrogance. I was unable to respond. This was an eighteen-year-old boy and there were two girls of eighteen and sixteen in the house. By the time all that a father like me could possibly think of rushed into my brain, he had stepped into the house. The potential danger from this made me follow him quickly.

The gentleman now occupied the west-facing chair, my usual seat, without even asking permission to sit down. Because I knew well that if I sat on any other chair in this house, it would be like a planet going off its orbit, I told him that the leg of that chair was broken, and pushed another chair towards him. When he moved there, I sat down on my special chair. That's a chair I used often—the weight of my bottom had formed a depression on it.

'Do you recognize me?' he asked, after he was sure that I had settled down in my chair.

'Of course. Aren't you the older son of Sankaranchetan of Thekkekoott?'

'Do you know my name?'

I was silent for a moment. Yes, I knew, but an unsure, anxious feeling, about how to say it, got stuck to the tip of my tongue.

'This is exactly my problem.' His voice rose a bit now.

'Santhosh, right?'

'Yes, but, Chetta, why did you take so much time to say it?'

Why was he here asking me all these questions when I had not, knowingly or unknowingly, done any harm to him, his father or their family. I sat there, not comprehending the situation at all, when the next question came: 'Chetta, when I asked you about my name, didn't you really think of the other name first?' If I said no, that would be a lie. And a quarrel would follow. Since I had been caught red-handed, I felt it would be better to just admit it, so I nodded weakly.

'That is my problem. I came over to tell you that.'

My thought was what would have occurred to anyone else: What was the big problem in it? But seeing that he was staring hard at me and crouching in the chair as if about to leap forward, I did not reveal it.

'I can't bear this any more! I must make a decision!'

I could feel my throat close up as his voice rose.

'How long can one put up with it?' He stirred in his chair briefly as he asked this.

'Chetta, do you really know my full name?'

It wasn't a good moment to reply: No, I don't because there is no particular advantage from knowing your full name, I didn't care to study it. I could perhaps try putting together the names of his father and family. But that could potentially lead to an explosive situation, and I would bear the brunt of it, so I made an attempt to escape via a quick lie: 'I can't recall it . . . now.'

'You won't, even if you try, so why try?'

'No, not that . . .' I stumbled, trying to get a hold on it.

Suddenly, all the sounds in the house became inaudible.

'Not just you, no one in this place knows me . . . not even my old man, I suspect.'

I did not let go of this chance to deflect whatever anger he may have against me to his old man: 'Don't say that, Santhosh. Won't Sankaranchetan know?' His reply was somewhat sad: 'Oh, he may have forgotten.'

If one did not grab him and hold him close before he jumped into this abyss of sadness, the chances were that his voice would grow shriller still and he might just raise himself up on all fours. So I leaned forward a little and asked: 'Santhosh, tell me what's wrong. Like the elders say, there's a remedy for everything!'

'I have stopped believing in that, Chetta!'

'Please don't worry, just tell me.'

'I want my name.'

'You already have one: Santhosh. It is a good name, isn't it?'

'No, it's not enough to be just Santhosh. I want my full name. S. Santhosh Nair.'

'Your full name is right here. Who's going to take it away?'

'That's only in the government documents! Now, did you know my full name, Chetta?'

'Santhosh, do you know my full name?'

The gentleman shook his head to say no.

'P. Ramakrishnan Nair. But you know me only as Ramu, right? That's how it is. You may not know other people's official names.'

'I know that. But people call me by that other name. What about that?'

Noting that his voice was going to get shrill again, I said: 'Santhosh Nair wants to be liberated from that other name. That is all that you want, am I correct?'

The gentleman now nodded yes.

'We'll find a solution to it. All right?'

After that nod, he was quiet for a while. Then he asked: 'Are you just trying to pacify me or have you thought . . .'

'From now, I will call you only by your full name, or maybe just Nair. Won't that do? Gradually, everyone will call you that.'

Feeling that he was somewhat calmer now, I slowly revealed my own anxiety to him: 'But why have you approached me with this now?'

'I thought only you can be trusted, Chetta. You're the only one around here who is sensible enough to understand what I say.'

It is true that I was a bit swayed by that praise. But I did not allow a single ripple of that pleasure to show itself. Placing myself inside a frame of seriousness, which I assembled with considerable difficulty, I agreed with his viewpoint: 'That's true. This is a rural place after all. Backward.'

'Didn't I study in the local school till class twelve? I was called by that name so often then! But shouldn't it be different now that I am studying in a college in town? It's been just a month, and I was setting up something with a girl from a good family and then everything changed. Yesterday she asked me, is your nickname *Ambedkar*? I felt I had been wiped off, absolutely. I turned invisible where I stood! I knew this was going to follow me, so I'd even set up a new nickname for myself—Nair Bhai—before I joined college. This is somebody's wily plan. He gave it to me nicely. Ah, I'll haul him up! But that's not the whole thing. After this, she made a statement—ah, anyway you don't look like a Nair! Chetta, imagine my state then!'

For a few moments, I did not respond. No use here of history, social science or politics. The only prayer climbing up and down the staircase inside my head was this: Let this gentleman leave as quickly as possible. Maybe he noticed that my silence was a ploy to escape from this situation, for his next question was: 'Chetta, will you help me?' For a moment I hid my misery the best I could and looked at him.

'Chetta, will you or will you not?'

It sounded like a threat at first, but when it struck me that he had nobody but me to help him, I took shelter under that feeling and said: 'Let us wait and see, Santhosh Nair!'

'No, it's not enough to wait and see. Tell me if it will work or not. Otherwise, I know what to do!' That was a threat to his tormentors.

I was a little frightened to ask him about what had happened in the past, but finally, haltingly, I did. With that inquiry, the history of Ambedkar arriving at Kudamaloor School unfolded like a mat unrolling. The first chapter began on Gandhi Jayanti when Santhosh Nair was a class 4 student. The day was unique because this time, not just Gandhiji but Ambedkar too came to school—in the form of students dressed up like them. Muhammed Sharif of class 4 A was Gandhiji; Santhosh Nair of class 4 B was Ambedkar. The dhoti around Muhammed Sharif's waist came loose and seeing Gandhiji in his underwear with the round glasses, the pappadams pasted on his head to make it look bald and the staff in his hand, everyone forgot that it was Gandhi Jayanti and burst out laughing. Even then Ambedkar stood tall and serious, holding the fat book in his hand and pointing ahead with the other. Gandhi did not go along with Muhammad Sharif, but Ambedkar accompanied Santhosh Nair. And gradually, Santhosh disappeared and only Ambedkar remained.

It was Babu Saar, from Kurupunthara, who had suggested that one of the students dress up as Ambedkar on Gandhi Jayanti. This Babu Saar was fond of modernist poetry, plays and such things; the other teachers viewed this as some modernist-style experimentation of his. Two years later, he was transferred elsewhere. Santhosh now believed that he cast him as Ambedkar and not Gandhi because of his dark skin, and not because of any facial resemblance. I tried to ask him if it wasn't better to regard it as an expression of a teacher's affection towards a favourite student, but he just wouldn't be convinced.

'Chetta,' he insisted, 'both this skin and this name are trouble for me. If this name did not hang thus on me, this skin would not have been such a problem,' he kept saying. 'That Kannan Chettan, from the Thekkedam family, is he not pitch-black? People call him Pillai-ccha.' He mentioned this as an example to show that just that name—Nair, Pillai—was enough to keep him safe from the colour of his skin.

Though I wanted to confess that I did not have the mental strength to restore his name and its caste-tail, since he threatened at least a couple of times to seek out that teacher from class 4, I was beset with fear. As if taking a precaution against something untoward, I sent him home, telling him to return after two days.

I discussed this affair with my wife and daughters. My wife's sole response was an unspeakable swear-word. My younger girl spat out a big cussword without caring in the least for the presence of her father. My older girl agreed with her mother and sister, and then told me in no uncertain terms—'If you take up such things, we are going to give you a piece of our minds!' They ignored my protestations that I had the greatest respect for Ambedkar and had read two of the three volumes of his *Collected Works*.

Two days later, Santhosh made his appearance again. My great luck indeed that my wife and the girls were away at a wedding; otherwise, I would have been in deep trouble. In the interval of the two days, Santhosh had consulted a lawyer about a legal remedy for his predicament. He had apparently told Santhosh that there was no such remedy as 'Ambedkar' was not an insult, so a complaint that the name was being used to make fun of someone would not stand in court. When he asked if it was possible to move court against people sharing the picture of him in the Ambedkar costume on social media, the lawyer told him the same thing. To cool his deep anger that there could be no recourse to law, I made him a glass of lemon juice and comforted him with these words: 'There have always been such stories. None of this is new. Haven't you heard people joke in this way? One name in place of another! And then people call you both. Isn't it wiser to just ignore it all?'

Santhosh sipped his lemon water slowly and asked even more slowly: 'Why should I carry the name of a low caste—a Pelayan?'

'Ambedkar was not a Pelaya, he was . . .'

But Santhosh did not let me complete my sentence. 'But he was the Pelaya of those parts, wasn't he? That's all I meant . . .' I noticed that his voice was going up and felt quite powerless to say anything more. For some minutes, we were both silent. Then, probably tiring of the silence, he said: 'That teacher . . . that sod who made me dress like that . . . Let me find out where he is . . .'

'Santhosh Nair,' I blurted, along with the fear that had bounded out from inside, 'please don't do anything drastic. We'll find a solution to everything.'

'Is that certain?'

I took both his hands in mine and reassured him: 'Believe me.'

After I sent him away, I thought: Why am I getting into this? It was perfectly possible to end it in a mighty bout of swearing like my wife and daughter. If I was still paying so much attention to it, I'd better find out why, I felt. At the end of the self-investigation, I realized it was because this was the first time in my life that someone was reposing so much trust in me. Even my wife and children do not trust me much. I am just a passive husband. A passive father. I am not valued beyond that at home. Nor have I desired more appreciation. Even if I desired it, I am not likely to get it. When such a person gets a chance like this one, it is hard for him to pull both legs out of it.

It was the feeling that there was nothing wrong in deriving a little pleasure from it that prompted me to go over to the president of the local Nair organization, the *karayogam*, without letting the family know. I presented Santhosh's problem before him, first extracting a promise that it would stay exclusively between us. He was a believer and a communist and, above all, someone who thought that because his father had written communist treatises, the ink had rubbed off on his bum as well. This respectable gentleman listened patiently and said, 'Surely this is an identity crisis. Everyone in this *karayogam* and in local party circles must henceforth address him only as Santhosh Nair or S. Nair or just Santhosh.'

The efforts he undertook on a war footing seemed to have had a positive impact, judging from Santhosh's beaming face a few days later. The suggestion that I had made, that those who had got used to calling him 'Ambedkar' could simply abbreviate it to 'Ambi', was also a partial success. But because he mentioned that the situation in his college and the budding romance deserved urgent attention, I took a few hours out of my day at work and paid a visit to Santhosh's college. He arranged for me to meet with the girl he liked. I was able to talk to her at length about Santhosh Nair's ancestry, about the chair in their family home in which the supreme leader of the Nairs, Mannath Padmanabhan, had once rested, and about how his folks were among the most blue-blooded families around there, and thus convince her, to some extent at least, about Santhosh's essentially pure Nair-ness.

In between, he told me that he had hired a few thugs to beat up those who had called him 'Ambedkar'. I declared to him that I did not believe in violence. But since I felt if the aim does justify the means then let it be so, I did not actively interfere in it. And I further advised him: If you dress up as the guru of modern Nairs, Chattambi Swamikal, for the annual day of the Nair *karayogam* next year, you can convert the 'Ambi' into 'Chatt-ambi' for good! Santhosh was inclined towards claiming the swagger that came with the literal meaning of the word 'Chattambi'—a goon, a violent enforcer—and was delighted that he could then take the title without actually engaging in violence.

And slowly he freed himself from Ambedkar and escaped into Santhosh Nair. It was on the day that he hugged me with joy, announcing this process to be complete, that I related the whole business to my wife and girls. They listened to it, but simply returned to whatever they were doing without offering an opinion or a single word of appreciation. The next day, my wife and two daughters left for her maternal house. They did not tell me why they were going or when they would return. They are not picking up the phone either. It's been two days now.

Now I am going to go over there. I am going to tell them that in truth it was Ambedkar whom I freed from Santhosh Nair. I can't think of anything else to say now.

Originally published as
'Malayali Memorial' in 2022

Kottayam 17

'Kunhucheta, are you taking a dump?'

Turning towards the voice that had came up the narrow lane on the other side of the tapioca patch and was now beside the fence, Kunhu replied: 'No, eda, I am manuring the tapioca.'

'What a crazy thing you did yesterday? You'd better put it back before it is fully light! If not, they are all going to come over here. And it will be a mess—police and everything—be warned!'

'Oh, really!' Washing his bum with a little water, Kunhu said, 'What if it fell ill from all that wind and rain? Would they have cared for it?'

'Uh! Do as you like!' Thankachan of Edathattil snorted. He walked away through the morning light that was becoming brighter still.

As he walked back home through the tapioca patch, Kunhu spotted a wilted tapioca plant that stood face down. 'What happened to you, old girl?' asked Kunhu, squatting beneath it. It stayed silent.

'Your roots aren't catching something?'

No, it shook its head.

Kunhu moved closer to it and said, 'God doesn't give everything to everyone easily. You don't worry, my girl. I promise, you're going to be the mother of all the tubers that grow around here, okay?'

The plant raised its head a bit and looked at Kunhu.

Kunhu sprinkled some of the water he had left on the plant and declared, 'I hereby wash away all your sorrows with this holy water. I baptize you!'

A whiff of breeze ran through, cutting through the tapioca patch quietly.

Pennamma stood leaning on the kitchen wall, watching the usual chattering and baptizing on Kunhu's way back. She knew well that by the time he finished paying a visit to the varikka, the jackfruit tree that was forever moaning about its impending death, and to the breadfruit tree that his grandfather had planted, the coffee would go cold. She hollered out to him: 'Can you hurry up?'

Kunhu was standing below the varikka tree, caressing a newly sprouted plant.

'Kunhe, didn't you hear, Pennamma's calling.'

Who's that, thought Kunhu, looking up at the tree. A chameleon. Hiding behind a jackfruit.

'Aha, so you are up there, huh?' asked Kunhu. 'What did you say?'

'The coffee's going to go cold if you don't hurry,' said the chameleon, slipping down to the lower branches of the tree.

'Oh, she's bluffing.' Kunhu squatted near the young plant.

Seeing Kunhu staying back under the tree and chatting to it, Pennamma stepped out of the house. She noticed the door of the shed open and went over to close it, saying, 'God, I closed this door last night!' She was just about it close it, when she turned back for a quick glance and shrieked, 'Good Lord!' Hearing her, Kunhu ran up as fast as he could, panting. She was shaking. Kunhu was confused. Her trembling fingers pointed towards the shed. Beyond her finger, on the floor of the shed, on two sacks, lay the holy idol of infant Jesus from the cupola down the road at the junction, swaddled in Pennamma's saree.

'What's this, Kunhe?' Pennamma asked.

'Oh, don't you recognize him?' Kunhe took her inside the shed. 'Our boy, of course.'

'Kunhe, please, please take him back to his house,' Pennamma said very slowly, her voice still quivering. 'If someone notices . . . that'll be bad enough . . .'

'Don't you want to keep our little boy here with us for at least a day, Pennamme?'

Kunhu's question made her burst into tears. The kohl that lined her eyes came flowing down like in a cloudburst.

'My dear, don't cry.' He tried to wipe off her tears, but Pennamma wailed like a child. Kunhu picked up Baby Jesus from his bed of sacks. They did not see how Baby Jesus was gazing at them.

Kunhu asked Pennamma, 'Don't you want to hold our boy?'

She held out her shaking arms and took him. She thought that a streak of lightning from her womb had struck the hard ground and cleaved the earth. She kissed Baby Jesus's forehead. Her tears slipped down to touch him; then they lay quietly there making little circles.

Pennamma brought a cane basket and gave it to Kunhu.

'Take him back in it.'

When Kunhu was about to loosen the saree in which he was swaddled, Pennamma stopped him. 'No, don't. What if he gets a chill?'

As Kunhu descended the steps towards the lane, Pennamma reminded him, 'Don't take the main road. Go by the buffalo-pen of the Palambadam house; take the tiny lane behind it. Please don't linger anywhere!'

Kunhu was turning the lane towards the Brahmin house of Thekkedathu Mana when Edapally Jose's son, Maathukkutty, leapt out in front of him, trying to scare him with a big boo! Just to make him feel good, Kunhu exclaimed, 'Ooh! I am so scared!'

A raw mango with a pointy snout was peeping out of the pocket of Maathukutty's knickers. Mango stains were evident on his chest and hands. A red ant was balancing on his head, tiptoeing on one strand of hair like an acrobat on a tightrope.

'No school today?' asked Kunhu.

Struggling to keep up with Kunhu, Maathukutty said, 'Oh, Kunhu cheta! There is no school today. Today is Sunday!'

Good God, today is Sunday, Kunhu remembered with a jolt. He ordered his legs to walk even faster.

'Kunhu cheta, what is in that basket?' asked Maathukutty.

'Our *kochu*—our baby,' said Kunhu.

'You'll let me see?'

Kunhu lowered the basket and moved the lid. Maathukutty peeped in, and seeing the face in that tiny darkness inside, asked, 'Sleeping?'

'Yes,' Kunhu said with a nod.

'Let me cover him again,' said Kunhu, 'and let us get going!' When they reached the yard of the Moolel family, Maathukutty said, 'Thaaa, Kunhu cheta, I am going over there,' and climbed up. Kunhu heard a Kappal mango tree tell a Moovandan mango tree that Maathukutty was coming that way. Kunhu stood there for a few moments watching Maathukutty get past the prickly thodali and scamper off like a rabbit.

As he walked on, he whispered a question into the basket, 'Boy, don't you also want to go picking the Kappal mangoes?'

On his way, the crow, the cat, the shoe flower and every other thing kept asking him, Kunhu cheta, what's in the basket? He told them all. Some wanted to go with him; he let them.

When he got past Ramakrishna Pillai's ration shop, Kunhu saw a crowd gathered below in front of the cupola. Their voices were cavorting together in the air above. The parish priest was standing in the middle, saying something to everyone. When they noticed Kunhu approaching carrying a round basket, they fell quiet. All eyes were now on him. Kunhu went up to them and lowered the basket to the ground. Then he glanced at the faces of everyone gathered there and opened the lid. Lizards and ants and chameleons and cockroaches jumped out as though it were Noah's Ark; they ran or slithered away through the crowd. When the creatures disappeared, they all saw Baby Jesus sleeping, swathed in a saree, on the manganaari creepers and hibiscus leaves.

'Son of a bitch,' shouted Devassy Parel raising his leg to kick Kunhu, but the parish priest stopped him.

'Accho, he needs a kick on his hip. Only then will this fucker learn.'

The priest told him to be quiet and grabbed Kunhu by his mundu: 'What did you think—that you can do anything dead drunk? Don't try to play around with the holy icon and the Church!'

Kunhu folded both hands respectfully and looked around.

'Accho, slap him hard! If you can't, then let us do it,' snarled Avarami Ottaplaamood.

Kunhu scanned the crowd once more and said, 'Accho, Thomachi, Avarami, tell me, what wrong did I do? Like every day I had my usual at Velachi's toddy shop, and then I was sitting right here, on the steps of this cupola, chatting with my little fellow . . . like I do every day . . . and then it began to rain *chara-para, chara-para*. Then, look, through that gap in the broken tile, the rainwater began to fall as thick as a pounder-stick on my boy's head! How could I bear it! What if he fell ill with a fever . . . yes, *vallo paneem pidichu kedennaalo*? So I kept drying his head, but the rain wouldn't stop. How could I leave him here with the water dripping on his head? That's why I took my child home. He slept well at home, covered in Pennamma's saree.'

'Oh, the icon's going to catch a cold!' Devassy muttered. 'The bastard's raving mad.'

'Accho, you shouldn't leave it at this,' said Vareethu Mappila. 'Tomorrow he'll take the icon home from the

Church and put it in his loo—and say that Christ wanted to take a dump.'

The priest looked at Kunhu. Kunhu returned the look.

'Either hand him over to the police; or you take a decision,' Vareethu Mappila urged the priest.

The priest was silent for some time and then warned Kunhu. 'It isn't that I don't know what to do with you. But as this parish includes you, the shame from what you do will fall on all of us here, and that's the only reason why I am not turning you over to the police. From now on, keep away from here—no more calling the holy icon koche and cooing to it!'

He ordered the sexton to place the holy icon back in the cupola. Kunhu begged the sexton who came to take the basket, 'Let me please see my child once more.' Someone grabbed him by the neck and shoved him hard. Kunhu fell down on the ground. Kochappi Manoonelle spat at him: 'Hey, a fellow who can't even knock up his wife is playing doll with the holy icon! Stop the nonsense! If your woman isn't getting knocked up, try tying her up in another cowshed! Maybe that'll help. Or I can come over when it's dark . . . Then you won't have to sit here cooped up, moaning koche, koche . . .'

Kunhu did not feel like going back home. He went over to the Reveeshwaram canal bank and sat there for some time. In the yard nearby, Nani Amma's cow was grazing. The crow that came and landed on her back whispered something in her ear. The cow looked at Kunhu sadly. Neither the cow nor the crow knew how to console him. After a while, Kunhu went to the toddy shop.

Beaten-rice seller Mammath came in there telling Velachi, 'Hey Velachi, don't give me the toddy that you gave Kunhu yesterday!' Kunhu was standing in the middle of the shop, drawing squiggles on the floor of the shop with his big toe. Mammath went up to him and asked, 'Kunhe, wouldn't it have been terrible if you felt like taking home the whole cupola?'

Kunhu looked at him and smiled. Mammath could not fathom what was in that smile. Seeing Kunhu walk out without drinking all of the toddy that he had ordered, Velachi called after him, 'Kunhe, *enna pokkaayithu?* What's up? Where're you off to?'

Remembering Achan's stern warning that he was not to go through the junction in front of the cupola, Kunhu went home walking on the ridge near the Parenkandam. On the way, the tailor Shantha's daughter, a third-standard student, saw him from afar and called out to him in her merry voice, 'Kunhu cheta, sing me that song again!'

Kunhu leaned on the fence and begin to sing:

The train ran fast on the river Parambuzha
That was way . . . long, way . . . long ago

And behind it ran Yesudas with his song
That was way . . . long, way . . . long ago
Oh what a fib that was, way . . . long,
Way . . . long ago . . .

Pennamma was sitting on the half-wall of the veranda waiting for Kunhu. He went in and threw his towel on the door. Then he lit a beedi and asked her: 'Did you go see Madhavi Amma of Akkarethaazam? Velachi was saying that she's been unwell.'

Pennamma paid no attention to what he said. She went up to him. 'Did Achan tell you not to take the road by the cupola?'

Oh, what wind or sun or crow or *maccachi* brought the news to her so fast, Kunhu wondered, looking around to find out. A *kuttathi* frog sat beside the well stealing glances at Kunhu. When Kunhu's eyes reached there, she quickly jumped into the well.

'What did Kochappi say about us not having children?' Pennamma sounded stifled.

Kunhu held Pennamma's hand. 'Oh, he just got mad and said some vague things. That's all right. God didn't give us that good fortune. Don't cry, my dear, just get me some coffee.'

They did not have supper that evening. They couldn't sleep either, so they sat together on the veranda, watching the dark. Pennamma saw the flame of a lit torch coming

94

closer and got up. It brought the grave-digger of the church, Paulose.

'Kunhe, I have to tell you something.' Paulose drew a line in the air with the flame of his torch. 'The Church committee met today and expelled you. You've been told not to go there too.'

The light that danced in front of Paulose and swayed behind him gradually disappeared; now darkness took its place.

The next morning, Kunhu, who was clearing up the ground below the banana trees, threw away his spade and ran towards the house on hearing Pennamma's loud cries. She had been sweeping the shed. He found her shaking; as he went closer, he too saw it. On the sacks that lay on the floor, a broken piece—a tiny finger! Pennamma looked at Kunhu, scared. 'Pick it up, Pennamme,' said Kunhu. Pennamma joined the little finger from the cold earth to the warmth of her body. Kunhu closed his eyes. The lightning that flashed overhead then pierced the space between the tiles of the roof and wrote on the air above their heads: Holy be to the father, and to the son, and the holy mother!

Originally published as 'Kottayam—17' in 2010

Moonlight

in

Human

House

I am the new occupant of this house. My parents and siblings were devoured by the tomcat from next door. I escaped somehow. When I fell off the loft, from that red cloth, that pretty lady who's all grey now but still thinks she is young, she's the one who saved me. When I scurry and scoot around her she throws me an irritated looks and says, 'Hey, you naughty boy, remember what'd have happened without me that day?' I am used to hearing this, so it makes no difference to me. I pretend not to hear her and dart around the room just as merrily as ever. But the lady won't give up. She'll keep muttering, 'You wait, the tomcat has his eyes on you!' This actually makes my little body tremble with fear. But I act like it doesn't affect me; I turn cartwheels on the floor, scamper up the table and get on the sofa in the middle of the room. That's an old chap, the sofa. Maybe because it is so old, its body has gone all soft. Sometimes, just to show that I am not scared, I jump or hop lightly on it. Then it tells me in a slow drawl: 'Hey, go slow, little one. It hurts.'

There's just one being who does not like my antics at all and who stares at me all the time—the clock on the wall that can never come down here. Then there's the rifle. He is held up by two nails. You can never tell when they are going to give way. Then it's going to be a pretty sight—back broken, on the floor. He suspects I want to see him fallen thus, so he keeps telling me: 'Don't strut about so much! I have finished off five people with a single shot!' Only later did I learn that all this was just a boast. The poor chap has not killed even a single ant. He just brags. Once I asked him, Why do you—someone who hasn't managed to scare even a tiny ant—claim to be a gun? I got a scolding that day from everyone and a strong warning never to ask such things. But I have doubts, often. And feel queasy if I don't ask. And anyway, I always blurt out my doubts despite myself, no matter how foolish they may be. They say that I am the reason why they are able to kill the time in their old age laughing and chatting—I give them the occasions. Otherwise wouldn't they have had to carry on silently in this abandoned house, staring at each other? That's why I keep zipping up and down all the time. I don't remember my parents very well. But when I think that I too had parents, there's a rush of happiness that I feel first; and then I feel the pain of having lost them. I don't reveal it to these oldsters; why make them sad?

A couple of the roof tiles are broken. It's through those openings that the sunshine peeks in, like crows throwing their slanting sidelong glances. On some nights, the moonlight peeps in too. I hide behind the bed or the table then. When the wind blows now and then, the hinges of the outer window mimic the tomcat in their creaking, scaring me. On such days, whatever I hear makes me freeze in fright. Everyone knows about this, and so they have all told the window to stop frightening me this way. It always agrees not to repeat it, but, after a couple of days, it inevitably starts again, only to apologize once more, claiming that it is terribly forgetful. So I never go near it. One day, I tiptoed to it and peeped out. Outside, under the mango tree, the tomcat was sleeping. At that moment I really wanted to hurl myself on him and tear him to bits. But I know well I can't do it, just impossible. Truth is, I have stuffed all these emotions inside me, and I can't even bring myself to weep. Even if I cry softly, the tomcat is sure to hear. And before I can blink, he'll be upon me. Though it never really liked me, one day, I asked the rifle mounted on the wall if it could help me finish off the tomcat. Its response was most unexpected—it broke into tears. A rifle weeping? A weeping rifle? I was astonished. I consoled it, went over to the sofa and sat on it. Nobody could sleep that night. As if some weighty sorrow had laid siege to us. When it was past midnight, the radio began to sing in a broken voice, with difficulty. It sang very rarely, and now its voice was really low. The meaning of the song was this: 'You are alone; so are we. But God awaits us with the oar . . .' I could make out nothing. Sometime that night the voice asked me, 'Do you want revenge?'

In between, I look at the world outside through the crack in the loft. I can then see the banana tree, the mango tree, the jackfruit tree and the sky. Also the boy and girl who come to water the banana saplings. I have seen them kiss in the shade of the banana trees. Probably news of my watching them must have got out—that's why a dried-up coconut frond fell upon the crack in the last windstorm and closed it. The envious coconut tree! I then began to sit in the darkness and think about my parents. I can only recall a thin, filmy memory—of two tiny eyes, one my father's and the other, my mother's. I had to know why my parents and siblings were gobbled up by the tomcat. No one would tell me. In the end, sick of my constant questioning, the almirah said: 'The rat is the enemy of the cat.'

I did not understand then what 'enemy' was.

'What wrong did my parents do to the cat?' I asked.

No one said anything in response at first. Then the lame chair that had lost a whole leg shook a bit and said, 'Your race nibbles fruits, destroys crops and spreads plague. They make nests in the smallest places.'

I felt sad, close to tears. I crept to a corner. They probably wanted to make me feel better, so they all said, 'You shouldn't feel sad! After all, you are the vehicle of Lord Ganapathy!'

That was news to me. I was hearing of this pot-bellied god with a trunk for the first time. I was elated for a short while. Imagining the strange-looking big-bellied god arriving grandly, resting upon the backs of my ancestors made me laugh. But before I finished laughing, I asked a big question: *If that is so, why are we treated like everybody's enemy?* No one expected it to pop out of my little mouth. They all glanced at each other's faces. No one said anything. That night, I lay curled up inside that red cloth that had covered me back then, like inside my mother's womb. 'Don't cry,' it whispered to me in a scared tone; 'if you cry,' the cat will hear you. 'What will I do if the cat frightened me in my dream,' I asked in a stuttering tone. 'Nothing bad will happen,' they all reassured me. I peeked upward through the eyelets of the netted red cloth. I saw the moon through the gap between the tiles. The rabbit on the moon winked at me.

Everyone complained I wasn't playful any more and that I had become a very serious person. Earlier, in the morning, as soon as I woke up, I would come and lie placidly on the table. I'd then get up and pace around, lost in thought. Then climb up to the loft, sit there for a while in the dark, thinking. This soon became my regular routine. So I believed they were right. Once, in the middle of this routine, I took a look at my face in the mirror without anyone noticing. 'It has become more serious and even more pointy for that,' declared the mirror without a twinge of reluctance. I was truly embarrassed. I begged it to keep that observation to itself, but that rogue of a mirror spread it all over. Everyone began to look at me with suppressed smiles. Seeing them look at me that way, I too began to wonder if my face had become even more pointy. Then, after some time, I grew weary of the grave expression on my face and pushed it away, telling it to get along, and hopped off merrily. Thus I once again became the old me.

In between all this, two rafters fell off the ridge board of the roof. A few more tiles fell off. The house itself began to admit that it had begun to lose its teeth. A couple of showers walked right in. The sofa got soaked. 'I am so cold,' it complained. 'My legs are cramping,' the cot moaned. The floor was wet. The house wept frequently—'some more strong winds, and I will collapse,' it said. We tried to comfort it, saying that it would be all right.

One noon, when I was napping, I heard someone open the door. The breeze plays those tricks sometimes— pushing and shoving in and then running out with equal frenzy. *That's how the breeze is*, I thought, and lay there, when I saw a whole bunch of legs walk in. And there broke out a terrible bout of talking and noise. It came closer. I ducked under the bed.

After the legs had left, I noticed a very strong change in the mood. Everyone had sunken into that old age that they had hitherto forgotten. All of them were hiding something. And the more they tried to pretend that nothing was amiss, the more they failed in it. 'If you get too serious, your faces too will become pointy like mine,' I joked. They tried to laugh at it.

This is our last night together. Tomorrow morning, men will come to tear down the house. 'They'll pull off my three remaining legs first,' the chair said, trying to smile. 'What will we be tomorrow,' they try to talk about it with the indifference typical of old age. All through, we try not to weep. They are all worried mainly about me. What will befall me, what would I do—this is what troubles them most. I too have taken some decisions. When everyone is gone, I will go straight to that tomcat. I will tell him, it is you who murdered my father, mother and siblings. You have to kill me too. Maybe he will not have the patience to hear me out fully. So my sentence may never be completed.

Anyway, let me ask the radio to sing a song. Let me romp around a bit listening to it. And prance. And turn cartwheels, and then, and then, and then . . .

Originally published as
'Manushyalaya Chandrika' in 2012

Three
Travellers

'Shall we take leave of you now?' Maria's mother asked the doctor. The doctor was drawing squiggles on the paper. He merely hummed, noticing that the first circle he drew was now smothered with many other circles, and it looked like a trap of some sort.

'So we need not come again?' she asked.

The doctor looked up. The woman was waiting for his response.

'Where is Maria?' he asked.

'Outside,' she said.

Maria was walking through the children's ward. She was chatting with those she knew and trying all sorts of mischief. When she reached the doctor's room, she ran into the nurses leaving after their shifts. 'What's the big happy thing today?' they asked her.

'We are going home!' she said.

'When will you come again?'

Maria did not know. She made them wait there for a minute and ran into the doctor's room.

'Amme, when will we come back after we go home today?' Maria's mother turned towards the doctor. He tried his best not to meet her eyes. She caressed Maria's head and said, 'Another day.'

Maria laughed and ran out.

'When is the train?' the doctor asked.

'Don't know.'

'Where will you wait till then?'

'In the railway station.' She picked up their bag. 'Maria loves to watch the trains.'

The doctor stored Maria's case sheet inside the drawer of his desk.

An ambulance rushed up the road behind them, its siren sounding like a prolonged wail.

'God is merciful,' said the doctor, but without sounding fully convinced of it. 'Miracles are not impossible.'

Maria's mother sat up in the chair. The doctor accompanied them out of the room.

'What to do with all these medicines now?' She pulled out the medicines from her bag and held them out to him.

He had no answer to that.

Maria was looking out of the window at the end of the long hospital corridor. She looked like a shadow framed against the daylight outside.

The doctor watched Maria and her mother walk away. The mother held Maria's little hand firmly. The piece of cloth thrown on Maria's head to shield it from the sun kept slipping off.

When they reached the railway station, they learnt that their train was late by two hours. Two hours? Maria didn't know what that was.

'What's two hours? she asked.

'A long time,' said her mother, walking towards the empty bench on the platform.

An engine went past them soundlessly. As it moved away like a head severed from its body, Maria's mother held her child close.

'Is it a long time now?'

No, the mother shook her head.

'When will "long time" get over?'

'When the train comes,' the mother replied, watching the engine turn a bend in the far distance, with a tinge of fear in her voice.

Rubbing her face on the loose edge of her mother's saree, Maria asked, 'When will we come here again?'

Maria's mother felt that the barbs of daylight were pricking her from top to toe. She held Maria closer to her.

'Your hand is very warm, Amma,' the little one said, pressing herself on that warmth.

She pressed her face on her mother's breasts and dozed off. Her little heart beat close to her mother's body.

When a freight train cut across the station whistling loudly, Maria woke up. She looked at it sleepily and began to count: one . . . two . . . three . . . Then she heard a teeny wail below the bench they were sitting on, and looked down. A tiny kitten. She fixed her eyes on the kitten and counted from four to hundred. Only then did she notice that the train had passed them and was gone. Maria had learnt to count only till hundred.

'Amme, what is this kitten's name?'

'Why don't you ask it?'

Maria smiled at her mother, slipped off the bench and squatted near the kitten: 'Kitty, what's your name?'

'Miao,' it mewed.

Maria turned and looked at her mother.

'What's its name?' Amma asked.

'Cat,' said Maria.

A crow flew down and perched on the branch of the tree nearby. Maria smiled at it. The crow returned the smile. Kaa, kaa, it crowed. The kitten smiled too, and went miao, miao.

'Our train is going to come,' Amma said, after she listened to the announcements.

'So it is a long time now, is it?' Maria asked.

She nodded yes.

The crow flew away.

'Let's take this kitten with us?' Maria asked.

Mother had to think in order to find a white lie that could make sense only to children. Then, kissing her on the forehead, she asked, 'Won't the kitten's mum be waiting for her at home?'

The train was not crowded. Opposite them sat an elderly man. When the train started moving, Maria pressed her face on the bars of the window and looked out. From below the many legs dashing up and down the platform, the kitten was looking at her. Maria waved to it.

'Next time, we must bring it with us,' she said. Her mother did not reply. She saw two frightened little eyes glinting in the distance.

Maria was lost in the sights outside for some time. Then her eyes fell on the traveller sitting opposite them. She was seeing someone with a luxuriant white beard for the first time. She liked his cottony beard.

She slid off her mother's lap and, though a little shy, went up to him. He smiled. Seeing his toothless gums between the white beard and moustache, she was surprised.

'Amma, this grandpa has no teeth!' she said, turning to her mother.

He chuckled gaily. Maria liked his laugh. It sounded like a tinkle.

He held her close and asked, 'What is your name?'

'Maria.'

'That's a lovely name!'

'What's your name, Grandpa?'

'Easo. Jesus!'

Maria laughed at the name. He laughed too.

'The Easo in my house is a tiny baby—Baby Jesus.' She cupped her hands to show him how little Easo really was. 'Just as tiny as that kitten!'

'And what about me?' he chuckled again.

She thought about it, and then, stretching her arms wide, she said, 'You are a bii . . . g cat!'

He threw his arm around her and laughed his ringing, pleasant laugh again.

Houses and trees and birds and human beings were rushing by.

'Where are you going, Grandpa?'

'Home.'

'Where is home?'

'Far away.'

'Where is far away?'

Maria pressed her elbows on his thighs and looked at him. He pointed his finger beyond the window,

'There, over there.'

The train was crossing a dry paddy field. The sky at its edges was now starting to fill up with red-coloured streaks, announcing dusk.

'Where's your house, Maria?'

'You know Ashraf's house? Just next to it.'

The train's whistle sounded just then. Maria leapt up joyfully, trying to whistle loudly, like another train. But her voice faltered. Unable to untangle it from her throat, unable to breathe, she hugged her mother suddenly. Her mother's face was teary; she held her child and kept whispering, no, it is nothing, it is nothing.

When darkness fell outside, they became more fearful. The dark scar that lay beneath the eyes like a crescent now threatened to smother the whole face.

After some time, Maria got up from her mother's lap, looking utterly drained. Mother kissed her cheeks and forehead. She went towards the elderly traveller again. It was then that she noticed the cloth bag next to him. She tried to peek at it.

Not wanting Amma to hear her, Maria asked him in a low voice, 'What's in this?' She turned around to check if Amma had heard her. Amma would scold her if she had. Don't open the bags of others, don't ask them things, she would tell Maria sternly.

'My work tools,' he said.

Maria did not know what those were. He opened the bag for her to see. She was seeing the things in it for the first time—chisel, ruler, hammer . . . Maria looked adoringly at them and their owner.

Lowering her voice again and making sure that Amma wouldn't hear, Maria asked again, 'Where did you get them from?'

He too whispered, like her, 'My father gave them all to me!'

She touched those magical things. They all looked like toys to her.

'What does your father do, my dear?'

'I don't have a father,' she said, without taking her eyes off the tools.

Maria's mother saw a group of people fly without wings in the breeze and reach the windows of the train. They looked inside and vanished in the dark. The first group was of people advanced in years. Then came young people, wounded soldiers, widows, little girls drenched in blood, and last of all, tiny screaming babies. Her lips began to tremble.

The elderly traveller asked in a whisper that only Maria could hear: 'Do you want to come away with me?'

Maria's mother pulled her away from him quickly. She tried to hug her child the closest she could. The gasp of her fear was now louder than the train's thundering roar. She lowered the shutters of the windows in terrible desperation.

The train gained speed, piercing right through the womb of darkness and sounding like an ever-lengthening wail.

'I'll get down at the next station,' he said to Maria's mother very reluctantly, in that low whisper.

Maria's mother felt the cold creeping over Maria's body.

Maria glanced up at her mother's face, smiled and said, 'Oh, Amma is crying!'

The train dashed on with an ear-splitting clatter, crossing a river.

Originally published in 2012

The

World

of

Creatures

My mother's brother, my Ammavan, was in the army. He's settled in Delhi; he comes home for a visit very rarely. And he never stays for more than a couple of weeks. But Ammavan called me the other day and told me that they are planning to move back home. They have a house here, an old one that his father-in-law had bought them a long time back. It was occupied for the last ten years solely by a caretaker, Uroos. Ammavan wants to refurbish the house and stay there. He gave me some instructions. He gave me these tasks because he knows I know his ways and habits quite well. I love to do such tasks, especially minor chores, for him. So I agreed happily.

I've been there only once. That time, I went with him. I was amazed by the sight of the big house and the huge yard that surrounded it. Now, standing here, I feel disappointed and sad. The weeds have grown so tall that the outer wall is almost completely invisible. The front

MALAYALI MEMORIAL

yard is smothered with wild grass. You can't bear to look at the backyard; it has become a jungle.

Thank goodness, the veranda and the half-wall are clean. The row of framed photographs that adorn the wall of the veranda is also neatly kept. Insects have made their nests in a couple of places on the ceiling. The more I look at the courtyard and the backyard, the more irked I get. Maybe one can make allowances for the neglect of the backyard. But what about the front yard of the house? An enormous variety of plants! The bougainvillea creeper has climbed on to the roof and spread all over the tiles, blooming prolifically! The place would have looked nice if these were cleared. But how is one to feel surprised? Entrust the place to an irresponsible fellow, and it can only be as bad as this! In truth, I am in such a mood that I don't know what I might do if I manage to lay my hands on him—that Uroos. I might even kill him! One can't help thinking such things when forced to wait for him in front of a gloomy house overrun by wild plants! That's not my fault. And if anyone thinks that it is, I honestly don't give a shit.

I hear the sound of footsteps outside. Someone's coming from the back of the house. It must be him, Uroos. What should I do when I see him? Roll my eyes in anger or call him a couple of names? Or, be more serious, call him close and cross-examine him briefly? The sound is near now. I continue to wait there with a

122

grave expression on my face. But it is a kid goat that has walked up from behind the house. It sees me and stops, continuing to stare at my face as though it knows that I am a stranger. Then it goes to the gate and slips out through a gap. I notice the gap only then. It seems to me that someone has deliberately cracked open that really strong gate of iron.

Sometime after the kid goat has left, a bitch and her four puppies come in through the same gap. They look like a small but disciplined public procession. They pay no notice to me and go off to the backyard.

After some more time, I hear footsteps again. This time it is going to be him—I was sure of it—Uroos. But though they seem to grow closer, the sound stops suddenly. I feel a twinge of fear. The plants and trees around the house are strangely still. The panikkoorkka plant next to the jasmine vine that I am facing seems to move briefly. No, I am just imagining it. I look at the ilavu tree. Not a leaf of it has moved. I notice an owl hidden in it. Its eyes are focused on me; that look is the empty stare of a blind man. I act like I don't see it and turn my gaze elsewhere sneakily. Suddenly, a crow-pheasant emerges noisily out of the verdant greenery. It feel like a drop of blood has dripped down from its deep red eyes. No other sound is heard for some time. Then, after a while, the dog and her pups march back to the front of the house and go out. The last of the pups turns around to look at me when it reaches the gate. I fling a small stone at it that I have been holding. It hits the tin box fixed on the gate instead. The gate cries out, sounding like a pup's squeal.

Then I hear the windows of the main room of the house open behind me. I start and spin around. Behind the double-line-like bars of the window, I can see two eyes. My fear becomes intense. I hold my breath and stare straight into them. The eyes quickly withdraw into the darkness. When I hear the sound of the door being unlocked and unbarred from inside, which falls on my ears like the sound of pots and pans crashing on the floor in succession, I can't help but leap up from where I am sitting.

A small, thin, ordinary-looking man came out. He was not strong, nor were his eyes cruel. He came up to me. It took me a few moments to come down the staircase of fear that I had ascended. He waited quietly for me to utter a word. I did not say anything. He invited me as though he knew everything. He showed me my room. I went in and shut the door behind me. Hearing someone knock hard at the glass pane of the window, I wheeled around. But it was only the light falling on the window pane.

After staying in that house for two days, I understood a few things, one of which was that Uroos did not speak. He just listened to whatever you said. Sometimes he nodded. At other times, he was like a dead man. I had to holler loudly at him then. Then his eyes would shake themselves awake, as if from sleep, and stare at me steadily. I feared that his eyeballs would pop out and float towards me, such was its intensity.

I found out that some women were coming in to cut grass and children were taking away fallen coconuts, all without permission. I asked Uroos about this but he had no reply. I told them, when Uroos was present, that I would break their legs if they came again. I could see fear on their faces, and the same fear was reflected on Uroos's face too.

I was not able to sleep for a single day since I came here because of the mice. On some days, the noise from the loft would subside quickly. Then there would be complete silence for a while. Just when I'd feel relief and begin to fall asleep, the mice would appear, running all over the table and the almirah. Sometimes they would even get into my blanket, rub their faces on my feet and scamper off. When I jumped up in fright and looked around, only their shining eyes would be seen.

As the first step in cleaning up the house, I decided to exterminate all the mice. I told Uroos to buy a mouse-trap. He did it promptly. That made me feel a bit confident that Uroos might be a decent chap and an efficient worker too. Maybe he had fought the mice for ten whole years and failed. Maybe that's why he was so keen to get the mouse-trap.

He placed a piece of tapioca or banana inside the trap. Every day, we found mice trapped in it. Uroos would take them away to be killed. But despite this, the mice infestation did not decrease. With each killing, more mice seemed to be born! Till some days back, they had some minimal respect for me. But now they seemed to stare hard at me nastily; they gnawed off the handle of my bag. This was revenge, I thought, at my efforts to eradicate their very race. But that did not free me from the trauma of seeing the number of mice increase with each killing. That's why I hid myself and watched Uroos kill the mice. He placed the trap on the half-wall behind the house, put a banana near the mouth of the trap, and opened it. The mouse ate up the banana like a seasoned criminal, coolly. Usually, a mouse that eats a poisoned banana walks a few paces and then collapses, dying. But this mouse ate the whole fruit, then turned to throw a grateful look at Uroos, smiled a mousey smile and made off happily towards the loft. Uroos was feeding them fruit and cereals each day and freeing them all.

Since I felt that life ahead was going to be as difficult as conquering an unknown land, I decided to continue the combat with the mice. I trapped the bond between Uroos and the mice and drowned it to death. When I killed the mice myself, more than the dying agonies of the enemy who ruined my sleep, it was the scared, child-like, teary expression on Uroos's face that gave me the bigger kick.

One day, I was taking a shower. There were voices outside. Must be the grass-cutter women or the thieving boys looking for coconuts, I thought. Today, if I catch them, I'll break an arm or leg for sure, I told myself. I couldn't make out what was being spoken; the voices were too low. I peeped out through the top of the bathroom door. There was no one out there. A cock was loitering around the side of the kitchen. I was seeing it for the first time here. Where did it come from? The rooms were full of lizards, spiders, cockroaches and even civet-cats, and goodness knows what other creepy-crawlies, and now this! It's going to dirty the yard with its droppings, and scrape and scratch everywhere. Look another way for a moment, and it's going to come inside and snoop around the house. Must get some poison to finish off all these creatures. When I was washing my hair, I heard talk outside again. That too was unclear. The cock was missing. Instead, there was a black cat lying there. It let out a profound miao seeing me.

I walked around the house a couple of times looking for Uroos. Though very hesitantly, I stepped into the murky-green wilderness that had swallowed up the yard. You had to make way, cutting the vines. As you did that, some plants and creepers would twist around your legs.

The air was full of scents. Suddenly something darted off from under my feet, scaring me. As I stood there petrified, it slid back with equal swiftness and turned to another direction. It was a wild hare! One can't say what else is going to appear from this darkness—snakes, mongooses . . . I began to walk back. Then I heard a cow mooing. When I went ahead a bit, there she stood, under the mango tree. Good God, how did this huge cow get in through that narrow gap in the gate? I was amazed. I went up closer noiselessly and overheard the same soft voice that I had heard before outside. I began to tremble. Someone was hidden behind the mango tree. I took a few cautious steps forward, hid myself behind the jackfruit tree and listened. Uroos was talking to the cow. It wasn't clear what. The cow was nodding stoically, like a philosopher. I felt fear and amazement at the same time. Suddenly, the talking was over. The cow went off the north side of the yard, its head bent in thought. I watched it go. In that stretch of the wall there was a gap large enough to let a cow in.

Two months have passed after Ammavan and his family returned and started living in this house. Whenever I came here to visit them, he would ask secretly—what did you do with that Uroos? Did you manage to get him to leave, or did you finish him off? What really happened was this: I had been dreaming of all the trees in the yard turning into valuable furniture of different sorts and the

yard itself becoming a sea of light, cleared of all unruly
growth, but Uroos was unable to pluck even a single leaf,
and so I sold all the trees in the yard to a sawmill. They
helped also by sending a few workers who cleared up the
wild. They chopped down the jackfruit tree first. When
they were cutting the trunk after having brought down
the branches, Uroos was cooped up, nearly lifeless, near
the kitchen.

It was on that night that I finally went to bed with
the feeling that I may be able to sleep well. When I had
barely fallen asleep, a strange noise woke me up. There
was no one around. A firefly drew a line of light cutting
across the darkness and flew out. When I went back to
sleep, I heard the same sound again. I got up from my
bed. Someone was standing outside the window. Seeing
just a figure silhouetted in the moonlight, I knew who it
was—Uroos. Why is he standing outside my room with
his back to me and face to the yard, I thought, first with
fear and then with amazement. I pulled out the sharp
machete from under my pillow. I did not how he was
going to attack me—maybe by smashing the windows,
or sliding down from the loft . . . I warned myself: do not
be frightened if he turns around and you find his face to
be that of a cow or a cat. After a long time, he began to
walk soundlessly towards the farther side of the yard.
Then, and only then did I notice—slithering, flying,
walking, innumerable living things were following him.

I went out of my room slowly. It seemed to me that an ark of green was carrying Uroos and other living things away, to some far place. As I stood there watching them go, the menacing shadow of an enormous bird hit me. I fell on my back, face up.

If I tell Ammavan this, he'll just tease me, saying that I'd made it all up. That's for sure.

Originally published as 'Pranilokam' in 2012

Multiple
Lives

What I am about to tell you is just an experiment. Imagine that three people are standing on the second floor of a building with five floors. Let's call them A, B and C. They are looking out, seeing the sights out there. Half an hour later, they are asked to write a short description of what they have seen. Their write-ups read like this:

A: The road was very busy. The vehicles were speeding. A senior man was waiting by the road, seeking a chance to cross it. Because of the busy traffic, he was unable to do it. The wall behind him, close to the footpath, was plastered with cinema posters. Many of the passers-by were looking at them. After some time, the senior pedestrian, probably tired of waiting, leaned back on the wall on the side of the footpath. The hope that some vehicle would slow down for him to pass had left his face. He turned around and began to look at the posters.

B: There was a police jeep under the signboard that said 'No Parking'. There was a man standing behind it. When he lifted his hands in between to scratch his face, the handcuffs on his hands became visible. Passers-by threw curious glances at him. A small group that was standing apart from him kept its eyes on him. He, however, did not pay any attention to them and kept scratching all over his body.

C turned in a blank sheet.

Is there anything interesting about this experiment? It is natural to expect answers to this question to be, Yes and No. But this rather unremarkable experiment has helped me gain clarity regarding some aspects of my life. On many days, when I read the newspaper, my attention slips quickly from the line I am reading to the advertisement in the next column, and returns to the line with the same speed. Likewise, I travel from the time and the place where I am right now to another time unconnected to the present, which is chaotic, disorganized, and which may be called absurd or mysterious. I'd be, of course, in the present—in this second-floor room, in this chair, immersed in my thoughts. It was when some people indicated to me that I sometimes said things that were absurd and out of place when everyone else saw the same things, heard the same sounds and enjoyed the same fragrances that I began to ask: Am I a multiple?

Multiplied by two or more? There are some things that happened in my life that made me feel so.

When the Soviet Union collapsed and everyone was sad and lamenting, I alone said that the real issue was that schoolkids would no longer get the shiny smooth pages of the Soviet magazines to cover their books with—that statement got me into trouble. On another occasion, while among those who were celebrating the anniversary of the October Revolution, my thoughts were of Lenin who was travelling from Zurich to Russia with his wife and lover to ignite the revolt, sitting with them on either side. When revolutionary slogans were raised to greet Comrade Lenin, my voice was the loudest. I waved my fist in the air with great fervour. I was there with the Russian comrades then. But I was also travelling, at that moment, with Lenin the husband and Lenin the lover.

I have already said that the above experiment gave me a measure of clarity. That is not related to these matters, about the fate of the Soviet Union and the October Revolution. But it is also related to them, in a way. My messy style and disorganized thoughts must have plunged anyone facing me right now into confusion. That's how I am. Or it's not my manner at all. Let me tell you of a recent experience. Maybe one similar to what I have been just relating. Since I don't want to create suspense like in literary writing, let me tell you in advance that what I am about to tell you does resemble the experiment that I told you about earlier.

There's a man who comes here regularly. His name is not relevant. Maybe it is deeply relevant to another person but as far as I am concerned, this man is just a 'he'. When he came here the other day, I requested him to look out through the window and give me an account of what he could see. Before he began his description, I turned my back to him and faced the opposite wall, closing my eyes.

This was his description: I see a lot of vehicles and human beings. It is bright and sunny outside, so many people are carrying umbrellas. A man is sitting all alone in front of the factory holding a flag up. He is young and wears a blue shirt. There's stubble on his chin. The factory gate opens now and then, and some cars come out. No one coming out or going in pays him any attention.

His account was almost solely about the young man who was on strike in front of the factory. After I heard his whole account, I asked him to take my position, with his back turned to me. I then began to describe the sights outside. Let me summarize it thus: I see a large window that opens to the outside. That's not a room, just a vast open area with a window. There is just a man and a woman there. The man is wearing a blue shirt. He has stubble on his chin. The woman is clad in just her undergarments. She kisses him from top to toe. She removes his clothes; he is now naked. A sea-crow circles the two in the sky for some time. The woman embraces the man. But he seems to have fallen into a very deep sleep even though he is standing erect; he is now snoring. Disappointed, the woman squats on the floor.

After I finished, I turned to look at the man. He was gritting his teeth in rage. Why was he so enraged, I could not make out. He leapt up and declared repeatedly, angrily, that the man I saw was not the striking worker. I saw that it was the physical similarity between the man I saw and the striking worker in front of the factory that riled him. He also accused me of deliberately projecting the image of the sleeping man on to him. Here is where I have always got into trouble. Such disbelief declares that all I see is unreal.

He came to me very early the next morning. I was sitting, looking up, doing nothing in particular. Though I say 'doing nothing in particular', I was not idling. He came to me and told me some things. His intention was to prove that my sights were unreal. This is what he said: things are not like what you see or think. That man is a worker with fifteen years of experience in that factory. Can you say that his efforts to counter the anti-human actions and positions of the factory management over so many years were all wrong? Was it wrong for him to demand that the workers should be given a least a small share of the enormous profit that the factory makes every year? Now he has been dismissed for trying to organize the workers against a move to sell the factory to some foreign investors. Can you say that a worker has no right to protest against foreign investment? Was it wrong to forewarn the workers that the new ownership may mean mass termination of employment? The factory management has filed a couple of false cases against him. His family is in dire poverty. Please stop abusing him.

What abuse did I hurl at him? I said nothing of that kind. Whatever I said was my truth—true as far as I am considered. For him, my words may be falsehood. I don't disbelieve anything he said. I know that the longstanding dispute between truth and falsehood has no relevance at all in this context. As far as I am concerned, the only small doubt I have had, then and now, is this: How is it that whatever I see becomes the real, and what another sees becomes the unreal? When I see a glass full of water, sometimes I see only the water. Sometimes I see just the glass. Is there any rule that you must necessarily see both? Is it not the fact that everything he said about the worker just now are but commonplaces? Repetitive, the literary critics would have said, if it were literature. Whether in real life, or in literature, I do not find it boring. Maybe it is boring for someone else. Is it necessary for me to tell someone who thinks so that they are wrong? I don't know. He kept insisting I see the truth and acknowledge it. He must have been so convinced that I would be able to recognize the truth that he was trying to point to me there. It is only the lack of humanity of the act of refusing such a man and disappointing him that made me go over to where he stood and look out of the window like he asked. But this is what I saw: a great crowd of people, men and women, old and young, gathered in front of a portrait of Stalin, all of them masturbating openly. Dicks, in men's hands, like blind fish coming up for air, peeping out. Women's fingers, like the food-filled beaks of mother birds, going in and out of nests. When I started describing all this, I heard the sound of something breaking. He had stormed out of the room.

Last evening, he came one more time. For a while, he just sat facing me, saying nothing. Maybe he was saying things silently then. I looked at him. I shrank into my own anxiety about what he was about to say. By then, however, I had also expanded into something else. It is said that writing about masturbation in literature is obscener than a word grown dim and dirty from overuse. But how can the sight that I saw turn into an overused word? Why is it that I worry so much in between about certain standards employed in literary writing? I know nothing of this. But I do know too.

Suddenly, he began to speak. He spoke without expecting any reply from me. And so, it turned out to be a long soliloquy. One that went around the world, touching political revolutions around the world, the history of the Soviet Union and imperialism. I am not surprised when such a person speaks thus. When I say that I indeed expected this of him, that's really not out of my egotism. Maybe someone else will see only vanity in it. Some circumstances are so easy to disentangle, like one is able to say if someone walked through such-and-such a road, he will reach such-and-such a place. That's probably why it is easy to predict that certain things will happen in their lives of the majority. I could guess what he would say after that historical exposition. And I was right: he said that the worker is near death now. His children too are ill and hospitalized. The factory management has not budged an inch. In two days, the foreigners will take over the factory. We will have to witness the whole family committing suicide.

When he spoke thus, I did not reveal my impatience even a bit. Nor did I point out derisively that such an ending was utterly predictable. But when he kept insisting that all that I saw was wrong, I wondered why he was so worked up. He then became adamant, and without a drop of tolerance, forced me to look at the world outside with him. But before I could try to convince him that there was no need to insist that only some particular news was to be noticed, that only water from a certain source should be drunk, only such-and-such a sight was worth seeing, I saw the expression of his face change.

His muscles were tense. When his hand tightened around my wrist, I felt the pain. I had indeed expected such a response. He must have become determined to end this child's game in which one person sees and the other sits with his eyes closed. Pointing insistently to the world outside, he said aloud: 'Look, open your eyes and look . . . Tell me if I am not right!'

This is where we have a problem. I can maybe say that I see the man who he points out to me, and his misery. But what if I see something else? Or, what if I don't see anything at all? Remember that experiment involving A, B and C? Not necessary to remember, of course. But I can see a few things: a crow is trying to balance itself on an electricity line; a woman is touching up her lips sitting in a car; someone just farted and is now closing his own nostrils.

He kicked me hard, called me a bastard and stormed out just because I told him that it was these things that I saw. If he'd kicked me harder, I'd have fallen off the second floor of this building.

Originally published as 'Bahujeevitham' in 2012

Possessed

'From today, the bank will make no compromise,' declared the zonal manager, Mr Anantharaman. 'We will be taking firm steps against defaulters. They will surely receive recovery notices.'

These words made Krishnan feel rather clammy and cold. Four ATMs, the crystal doors of the main office worth lakhs, the head of the senior manager, George Joseph—all these had been smashed in the name of political correctness. When Anantharaman began to argue that these acts were not the least justified, Krishnan was assailed by an uncontrollable desire to start booing. In the beginning, it was just a minor feeling but it soon threatened to grow into an enormous window-smasher of a catcall; stuck inside, it was nearly breaking his vocal chords. When he felt that he could no longer hold back, Krishnan ran out of the room, knocking down several chairs on his way out. His colleagues, employees of the bank, were startled, petrified, as though they had witnessed something forbidden. Krishnan shut himself up in the nearest toilet. Rajendran, who had followed him, knocked on the door and kept asking anxiously if something was wrong. Inside, Krishnan was trying desperately to choke the sound, clapping both hands firmly on his mouth.

When the sound began to push upwards again, Krishnan thrust his fingers into his throat and began to vomit. Not just the idli and sambar from breakfast, but even the remnants of last night's chapattis and dal spewed out of his mouth. When the vomiting trailed away into a guttural noise, a thin ribbon of saliva connected Krishnan's mouth with the dirty bowl of the washbasin. He cut that ribbon, washed and came out—to face everyone who'd gathered there, with the same anxious expression on their faces. 'Nausea,' he told them.

'You didn't have breakfast at home?' Rajendran asked.

'No,' Krishnan lied.

'It must be food poisoning, please take care,' someone said.

Krishnan nodded. When everyone left, Rajendran asked, 'Are you feeling ill?'

'No,' said Krishnan, 'It'll be okay.'

'Saar, the way you ran out, I think everybody was dispirited, not just Anantharaman Saar.' He sounded a bit disappointed.

Krishnan did not reply; he went towards his cabin. There, forgetting all that had happened, he called his wife and told her that he would be back home early, and that they could go out together.

But he reached home very late that day. When she saw him, she burst out: 'I've been waiting here all dressed up fancy, did you notice? I should have known, this is how you are . . .'

She stormed away into the bedroom. There was a lizard on the wall, a few mosquitoes, a moth that was hitting its head hard against a patch of brightness near the tube light . . . *They are all throwing sidelong glances at me*, he thought. He ignored them and followed her.

'There was a small problem . . . that was why . . .' When Krishnan began to explain, Padmini got up from the bed and went into the kitchen.

Confused, he sat on the bed. He noticed a lizard peeping at him from behind a calendar hung on the wall. He stared it down and got up.

Padmini had got supper ready. Seeing her sit at the table like she was guarding his food, he was amused. But he did not smile. Maintaining a serious expression, he sat down on a chair by the table.

'Please don't fuss without knowing what happened?'

Padmini paid no attention. 'Something that should never happen in a person's life . . . that too . . .' Krishnan

147

did not complete his statement. He leaned back on the chair.

Turning all the irritation at being made to wait so long into worry as soon as she heard his half-finished statement, she asked, 'What problem?'

'Please keep it totally to yourself?' He lowered his voice.

'Tell me what happened?'

'Our Rajendran . . . you know what? He did something terrible in office today.'

'What did he do?' He saw the anxiety spread on her body as a shudder.

'Ah, how am I to begin?' He sported that totally unnecessary seriousness on his face.

An ant that had been circling the dinner plate now climbed on to Krishnan's hairy wrist. Krishnan chuckled and showed Padmini the wrist upon which the ant was running as fast as it could.

'Maybe this ant thinks that it is inside a jungle?'

'I have a hundred things to do! Stop trying to fool people,' she snapped.

He stopped her fingers that were extended with the intention of crushing the ant to death and helped it slip under the table.

'Padmini, please be calm! Everything has its own pace!'

'If you intend to tell me anything, do it quick,' she retorted, with a sharp look.

Krishnan swallowed a mouthful of water and started as if he was going to tell a story. 'Today we had a meeting with the zonal manager, Anantharaman Saar. When he was declaring that the assets of debt defaulters would be recovered, our Rajendran jumped up and fled. We were all shocked, stunned. I went after him. He shut himself up in a toilet. After some time he came out, soaked in sweat. When we all asked him what happened, he said that he felt nauseous, that's why.'

'Making up excuses for coming home late!' Padmini was angry now.

'He was actually just making up an excuse.' He sounded like he was whispering a secret.

'Then?' Padmini's eyes opened wide.

'I had got out early.' He swore an oath of truthfulness, putting his hand on her head. 'I swear on you! He took me to the Coffee House saying that we needed to talk about something. He started with some stuff at the bank. Then he came to the point. I still can't believe it . . . it was not out of nausea that he fled.'

'Then what was it?' There was fear in her voice.

'He apparently wanted to hoot the manager!'

Padmini looked at him in disbelief. Her chest heaved as though indicating the rise and fall of her fear. Since she could not believe that a man so well-schooled in social propriety could want to boo and jeer, she asked him once again: 'Are you sure you are talking about our friend Rajendran?'

Krishnan nodded to say yes.

'Why did he feel so?' Padmini's question still carried a tremble. Krishnan threw up his hands, signalling ignorance. He got up and went over to the balcony. Padmini looked at him stand on the margin that divided the well-lit home and the darkness outside.

* * *

'Saar, how are you?' The security guard asked him as he entered the bank.

Now every single mouth in this place was going to ask the same question. So he had an answer prepared for everyone.

'Food poisoning. The Udupi Hotel chap cheated!'

When a discussion on the quality of food served at Udupi Hotel started off from the far end of the room, he went to his cabin.

'Would like to see you when you are free,' Krishnan sent a note to Rajendran through the peon. Rajendran came at once.

'What happened?'

'A minor issue. But not really a small one.'

'Tell me, Saar.' Rajendran sounded keen to know.

Krishnan leaned towards him and lowered this voice.

'This must stay only with you. Not another soul should know.'

'No, no one will know. What is it?'

The natural curiosity human beings feel towards secrets enveloped him.

'This is about a college professor, my neighbour. Very good man. Helpful. Calm, good-natured, all that. He came to see me at home this morning.'

Rajendran leaned forward as though drawn magnetically; he and Krishnan were really close to each other now.

'The other day, when the PTA meeting was happening, our professor was gripped by a terrible urge . . .'

Krishnan glanced at Rajendran before he completed the sentence.

'What urge?'

'To hoot! Loudly!'

Fearing that Rajendran's eyes, which looked like they were ready to pop out, might actually brush on his face, Krishnan leaned back and began to tap on the desk. Rajendran was quiet for a while. His face looked like someone's who'd come back from death, and not able to come to terms with it—uneasy. Then he too lowered his voice and asked, 'And then?'

'Nothing happened. He managed to somehow suppress it. But that's not the issue now.'

'Then?'

'What if this recurs during a class or maybe at a crucial faculty meeting with the principal?'

'Yes, yes,' Rajendran agreed. 'Just imagine if we were to feel such an urge even when we are sitting here? God, it would be terrible.'

That made Krishnan feel that he was going numb in the back of his head.

That day, Krishnan reached home very late. 'Can't you call if you are going to be really late? Don't make those who are at home sick with worry!' Padmini complained as she opened the door.

'Don't you know, if I don't call, there'd be a reason.'

Padmini just looked at him. He handed over the vegetables and said, 'I was with Rajendran all evening.'

'What happened?'

'Ah, nothing much. I left office a bit late. And was on my way back after buying vegetables, then it happened.'

Padmini clung to him, looking scared.

'When we reached the front of AKG Centre, the party leaders were all coming out. When he saw their white shirts and mundus, Rajendran looked a bit mischievous and whispered to me, "Look at the white-painted tombs!" I liked the joke, but did not smile and retained my serious face. When we walked on a bit, Rajendran flung down the bag he was carrying and rushed into a by-lane. I picked it up and ran after him. There he was, with fingers thrust into the mouth, eyes bulging and making guttural noises, his body taut! His face looked so distorted then, like that of a wild animal!'

Padmini seemed breathless, her back pressed against the wall. He saw her breaking out in cold sweat.

When they went to bed, Padmini asked, still sounding scared.

'What if that Rajendran had booed aloud there?

Krishnan held her body, which was now nearly feverish, close. He asked her, 'Have you heard of Auschwitz? Buchenwald?'

No, she said, closing her eyes. Not wanting to hurt the innocence in that reply, he told her, 'Then sleep well.'

Rajendran came into Krishnan's cabin saying that he did not sleep a wink the night before. Krishnan was trying to save a butterfly trapped among the files.

'Saar, how is the professor?'

'Ah! A minor issue . . .' Krishnan opened the window and let out the butterfly that was perched on his finger. Watching it fly away, Krishnan continued: 'Yesterday we had gone out together to get some vegetables. The road was all blocked with the RSS route-march. We couldn't cut across the road before it ended. So we were waiting there for it to get over, when the professor dropped his bag and ran into a lane nearby. I picked it up and ran after him. There he was, with fingers thrust into the mouth, eyes bulging, and making guttural noises, his body taut! His face looked so distorted then, like that of a wild animal!'

Rajendran was silent for a few minutes. 'If he had actually booed loudly then . . . I can't imagine what . . .' Krishnan could sense fear in Rajendran's voice.

Krishnan did not reply. He merely looked out at people moving around outside the cabin.

'Saar, I know a psychiatrist. Why not consult him?'

'That's good, but . . .'

'What but? Even kids no older than LKG level are taken to psychiatrists these days.'

Krishnan agreed with that statement.

'I can book an appointment, maybe?'

'No,' said Krishnan, 'not necessary.'

Before he left, Rajendran said, 'Saar, when I was thinking about all this yesterday, I too felt like booing and jeering loudly. If you think about it a bit, you'll feel the same too; your mouth will start aching to boo!'

'I am here not for myself.' Krishnan told the psychiatrist. 'I am here for a friend.'

'What is the problem?'

'He's struggling with this crazy desire to catcall or jeer loudly when it's a really solemn moment. The other day when he was watching the Independence Day parade with his family, when he passed by the venue in which Indira Gandhi's birthday celebrations were on, and on other such occasions.'

'What is his background?'

'He is from a middle-class family. Harmless man. Reads a lot of history. That's his only quirk. No bad habits. Works hard.'

Finding some pills in Krishnan's pockets, Padmini asked, 'What are they?'

'Oh . . . they are Rajendran's,' he said absently.

'Why are you carrying them?'

'How is he to take these home? What if his wife gets to know?'

'If he is nuts, he must get himself treated, that's all . . . Instead of doing that . . .'

Before she could complete what she was saying, Krishnan forcefully flung the glass tumbler that he was holding. It hit the wall and shattered.

* * *

'Saar, how is the professor?' Rajendran asked him quietly.

'He took his pills for a couple of days but has stopped now. He says that if we let go of unnecessary memories and just mind our own individual business, it will all be fine.'

Rajendran looked relieved. He smiled.

'Yes, that is detachment, Saar.'

Krishnan felt admiration and respect for Rajendran. Rajendran felt somewhat shy and humble.

That evening, Krishnan and Padmini bought a dozen glass tumblers in place of the broken one. They ran into Rajendran and his family in front of the Coffee House. They chatted for some time and then split.

'No one can tell he was so unwell,' remarked Padmini when they had gone.

Krishnan smiled.

When they were having supper, suddenly, as though she were waking up from sleep, Padmini asked Krishnan: 'You asked me once about some . . . wald, what was it?'

Serving her the chicken curry, he said, 'Auschwitz and Buchenwald.'

'Ah, right,' said Padmini, tasting the curry.

'Those were high-end hotels in Germany and Poland, a long time back. Only Jews were allowed to stay in them,' Krishnan told her, squashing an ant that had climbed on to his arm.

That new knowledge made Padmini happy, and she ate really well.

Originally published as 'Bhoothaavishtan' in 2012

Detective

Ammumma

'Hey, boy,' Granny—Ammumma—called me to her side. 'Do you know what we haven't had in these parts even after all this while?'

I was hurrying out to take a dump when this puzzle hit me. I squatted, feeling sad that Granny continued to call me 'hey boy'—*eda cherukka*—even though I was now a full-grown man, back home for vacation, and she had no qualms about it at all. Sitting on the pot, I put aside that sadness and began to think about her question. What could that thing be? Abortions, elopement, gossip, quarrels, spats—all of these things existed here, just like in other places. What other things had we missed? My bowels were now empty but I was still thinking. Acchan came to the door and asked, 'Are you done, eda?'

Now what is THAT? I kept thinking of it and paced the house. Then I gave up and went to her. Granny had her seat behind the house, in a little veranda, on a wooden chair. She sat there all day long. I looked for her there. She was not to be found.

'Amme, where is Ammumma?' I called to her.

'Not in the veranda?'

'No.'

Amma came out holding a flat spoon. A curl of steam rose from it, giving up a faint aroma.

'You were sautéing the avial?'

She hummed, 'Yes.'

'Please add some jackfruit seeds to the avial!'

'Oh, really! Where to find jackfruit in July?' Amma was irked. 'Go and see where Ammumma is?'

What's wrong with these jackfruit trees, why can't they make fruit in July, I wondered as I went in search of her.

'Eda,' Amma called out to me after some time. 'She's over there.'

I looked in through the window—Granny was in the room, and she had bolted the door.

'If she sees you watching her, she'll start a row!' Amma warned me. 'Make sure she doesn't notice you.'

'She may be ninety, but her eyes are as sharp as ever,' she continued 'Don't make her give you a piece of her mind.' Amma went back in. That flat spoon was missing from her hand now; the aroma had disappeared too.

I wanted to call out to Ammumma and ask what was that thing that we lacked even now. But if I asked her now, I'd be showered with the choicest expletives. And she would never tell me, too. So I decided to be patient and hid myself behind the window. Granny was taking out all the books she had stored inside her mundu box. In my memory the books inside her box were of the same number—neither more, nor less—always. She never lent any of them. When I was small, I once asked her, 'What are you reading, Ammumma', and got caned hard for it. I went weeping to Amma, and she told me, 'Never ask Ammumma what she is reading. She just can't stand anyone asking that.'

* * *

I was eight years old when I discovered this mysterious thing that she kept locked away, carefully wrapped up in newspapers, and read by herself, refusing to share it with anyone else. The house was empty that day. Father, who was in the army and had been home for his vacation, had gone back. Amma and Ammumma had gone to attend the funeral of one of my father's relatives. I walked around the house, made sure the house was completely empty, and then went into Ammumma's room. It was hard to pull the two halves of the wooden door together; the stubborn thing finally came around after much effort. I closed the windows. The room became somewhat dark. But my keen eyes could find things with very little light, and soon I fished out the key to the mundu box from under the cot. I opened it. Long mundus were neatly folded and stacked

inside. I pushed them aside gently and found books—
many books. I didn't have the time or the guts to go
through them in detail, so I took a quick tour. They were
all covered and labelled; I memorized the names written
neatly on the covers. The sole familiar word among them
was 'Kottayam', which was part of a name. As for the
rest, I wasn't even sure if it was the name of the author or
the book. But there was some tune or rhythm to them—
that was why they stayed with me long after I had closed
the mundu box. I began to chant them when I was by
myself. Neelakantan Paramaara, Hariharan Paramaara,
Kannadi Viswanathan. Whenever I would see the name
of the place 'Kottayam' on bus-boards, I'd complete it:
'Kottayam Pushpanath'.

Though I learned the names by heart, I did not know
what was in the books. Only a funeral could possibly
get both Amma and Ammumma out of the house. I was
not taken to funerals. That's how I started praying for
deaths and funerals during the evening prayer.

*When Yama comes, throw him a glance from your
blazing eye.*

So that my fear of death is driven away . . . I thought
myself in a position to put in daily requests for the demise
of at least one acquaintance, but to no avail. But one
day, two people ran into our house early in the morning,
crying aloud for Ammumma.

'Ammini Amme, please come at once, save us!'

She was with my mother in the kitchen. It was a holiday and so I was snuggling inside my blanket. But when I heard this, I leapt out of bed and ran outside. Both were women. One of them was wailing non-stop; the other woman was alternating between talk and tears.

'Ammini Amma, save us! That hussy has left us!' said the wailing woman in between her cries. Ammumma was nodding, listening to them.

My mother brought them fresh coffee. They blew into it before taking a sip.

'How old is the girl?' asked Ammumma.

'Sixteen last Medam,' said one of the women.

Ammumma was quiet for a few minutes. Then she turned to Amma, 'You come with me.'

'The boy?' Amma asked, meaning me.

'Ooh! No *maakaan* is going to come and get him!'

Amma got me some breakfast and told me, 'Stay out of trouble and be quiet till I am back.'

'Where are you off to?' I asked.

'Do we have to take your permission?' Ammumma shot back.

As they were leaving, I asked Amma secretly, 'When will you be back?'

'This boy needs a good hiding,' Ammumma declared in front of everyone, gritting her teeth.

'Is this Radha's son?' asked the woman who had been wailing earlier.

'No, this is her son,' Ammumma gestured towards Amma. 'Radha has two girls.'

'Eda, don't go off to play somewhere leaving the house open,' Amma whispered to me.

I was sure Ammumma had heard that too. She was like the crow—Pappoottan, who came to clean our yard, used to say. She'd know if there was the smallest movement.

When they had all left, I drew a deep breath and went into Ammumma's room. I shut the door and windows. Now the door knew me better and did not offer much resistance. I opened the mundu box. Took the books out. Examined each one. Had some trouble trying to figure out a name she had written on each of them. It was fun to try and catch it—it would slip away each time I tried. Finally, I wrote it down: Detective novel.

Though I did not know what it was, the excitement was like that of meeting a white man for the first time. I savoured bits and pieces of this white man of a detective novel for some time. In between, Pennamma Chechi from next door came over to get the kanjivellam, the starchy water drained from the cooked rice.

I had barely heard her footstep before I leapt out of the room.

'Boy, where did your mother and grandmother go?' she asked.

I gave her question some serious thought and said, 'Detective novel.'

She looked at me, muttered something and went away with the kanjivellam. I stood there covered with the glory of having uttered a big English word.

When Amma and Ammumma returned, it was past evening. Ammumma did not come in; she went straight for her bath. Amma had probably missed my usual fuss and complaining, so she asked, 'Why, boy, why are you so quiet?'

'No, nothing,' I replied.

Granny called to her from the bathroom—bring me my bodice please—and Amma went to get it to her. I heard footsteps outside the house. When I went to see who it was, I saw a man standing outside. He had tied a towel around his head.

'Is Ammini Amma at home?' he asked.

The smell of bidi stepped up before the question itself. I took it in as deeply as I could and let him know: 'She is having a bath.'

Amma heard us and came out. Seeing him, she removed Ammumma's bodice from his sight.

'The girl was somewhere in the eastern parts, like Ammini Amma said,' he said.

Amma asked him to wait. I hung back there, enjoying the bidi smell that wafted in the air whenever he opened his mouth. Amma came back in a few minutes.

'Amma's told me to tell you to search her waist before she gets back inside the house.' He nodded in agreement.

'Some woman should search,' my mother added.

He agreed to that too and waited a bit to know if there was anything else. The scent of the bidi lingered for some more time after he went away.

I followed Amma and asked her: 'Where did you two go today?'

Amma did not reply; she went off to the kitchen. I went after her asking, 'Who's that man who came?'

'What's wrong with you, boy?' That was almost a roar. We both jumped. How did Ammumma, who was in the bathroom, reach there so quickly, so quietly? As I stood there frightened and balancing the scent of her oil on the tip of my nose first and then drawing it in, she told me to hold out both hands. She peered hard at them, touched them. My fingers trembled lightly. I could feel my hands fly towards her, like those of the Iron-Hands Wizard, the hero of Kannadi Viswanathan's novel.

Amma held out the bodice, probably noticing Ammumma's huge breasts shake under the towel she wore. She ignored it.

'I'll never do it again,' I said tearfully.

I knew that Amma was waiting, scared, outside because she kept saying, 'Amma, please don't hurt him' in a teary voice. When my crying climbed higher, her entreaties and sobs would grow even louder. Ammumma paid no attention to it.

For many days after this, Ammumma would not speak to me. I fell ill with fever a few times in this period. Ammumma was a secret worshipper of famed sorcerers like Kadamattathu Kathanar and Puliyaambulli Nambutiri. People say that she had learnt many tricks that way. Amma would say that even the bouts of fever that felled me in this period were her doing. When Acchan came home from the army for his vacation, both fell at her feet, begged forgiveness and beseeched her to heal their son. Ammumma apparently did not say anything to them then. That night, however, she called me to her and said, 'Your digestion isn't right. Don't eat whatever you find.'

She was talking to me after a very long time. The smell of the ayurvedic medicine Amrithaarishtam was all over the place then.

'Eda,' I turned, hearing the slow voice.

It was Amma. She had come back after a bath.

'Your grandmother is not out yet?'

'No.'

'What is she doing?'

'Looking through the old books.'

'Goodness knows why she needs them in this ripe old age?'

'She might need them for something?'

Amma hummed indecisively and was about to leave. 'What's this soap, Amme?' I asked her.

'Your father brought it from the army canteen,' she said. 'What about it?'

'Nothing,' I said, 'The older scent suited you better, Amme.'

She did not reply.

That day, in the evening, I went to the temple with Ammumma. On our way back as we neared the abandoned well near the school, she asked, 'Did you find out the answer to the question I asked you today?'

She was like that sometimes, spoke very formally. It wasn't necessary to ask the question with such formality. I did not respond. Ammumma didn't care that I was now a grown man and that I was working, and so on. You could never predict what she would say. I decided to be silent.

'You're such a big and important fellow now, but you still can't answer it?'

'No,' I responded quietly.

She threw me a look. Seeing the fear of her which was perpetually in me, she said, with utter ease, as though she were merely picking up a fallen leaf: 'There has never been a murder in these parts until now.'

For a moment, I stood rooted on the spot. I did not ask her anything. She probably didn't expect me to either. She just walked towards the path where the darkness was beginning to fall. I walked behind her. I felt that I should ask: isn't it a good thing that no one's been murdered here ever. I came close to asking her, but then I saw that she wasn't very visible in the dark.

After supper, I went to her and asked, 'Did you read the book I got you last time?'

'The fat book, you mean?' She was rolling out her mattress, preparing to go to bed.

It was then that I remembered that I had actually meant to ask her quite something else. When I said yes to her without thinking too much, she just showed me the big toe of her leg. It was bluish. I stood there silently, and she said, 'It was too heavy for my hand. Lucky, just a bruise on my toe. Could even have killed me!'

I had brought her that big collection of translations last time I came, wishing to add *Agatha Christie's Collected Works* to her reading at this late stage of her life as a reader. She probably didn't say anything then because it was my wife—she's from Manipur—who had sent it as a present. I remember that she had accepted it smilingly. Long back, when I had got my first job, I had bought her a set of classic writings by such luminaries of Malayalam literature as Thakazhi and Karoor with my first salary. When I gave them to her, she said something that sounded like a slap: 'So you are trying to improve me, eh, with high stuff?'

I was upset by that response, actually speechless. Noticing it, she turned a bit soft and told me: 'I need something to get me high in a story. These chaps can turn anything into a story. I don't like that.'

Handing back the books I had bought her with so much love, without a trace of regret at doing it to her daughter's son, with absolutely no tact, she declared: 'Someone is always standing in the dark. Someone else is seeking them out. That's what makes a story interesting.'

I knew she had filched that sentence from some novel. I didn't ask which. I had seen some notebooks in her box in which she had copied some such sentences and also tried her hand at writing detective stories, which were mostly half-finished. I did not show any surprise at this expression of hers, either. Probably seeing my feeble state as I began to leave the room, she told me: 'Once, four of the last pages of the detective novel I was reading were missing. The very pages on which the culprit's identity was revealed! But I am still high when I remember it. I had guessed who it was. But what if the writer had pointed to someone else? I decided that it wasn't necessary to know. I have that sort of engagement with this sort of book. Some, I don't finish—I find out the criminal on my own. I never read the last pages!'

I threw another look at the bluish Agatha Christie-bruise on Ammumma's toe and switched off the light in the room and from the past.

I went to my room and to bed. But sleep evaded me. How had the question that I wanted to ask Ammumma disappeared from the tip of my tongue? I just couldn't wrap my head around that. Instead of asking her if it wasn't a good thing that no one was ever murdered in these parts, and if the rest of the world too shouldn't be that way—that is, instead of sharing some of my thoughts about the world itself with her—I had asked her about Agatha Christie's books. Why did I ask about just the books? Was it because my fear of her had driven the words back into my mouth, or because I believed, at the level of the unconscious, that the safest path was to talk about books? As I tossed and turned with these thoughts, I encountered a serious feeling: that my grandmother regretted that we had not yet faced a calamity. Yes, I felt sure. As I kept strengthening that certainty, I drifted into sleep.

I woke up late the next day. There was no one at home. People were hurrying through the lane in front of the house. I went out without even washing my face to find out what the matter was, and found Amma and Ammumma come up the steps from the lane.

'Where were you?' I asked.

Amma came up close to me and said, 'Our Soman Nair—found dead on the ridge by the side of the Reviswaran paddy field!'

I turned to Ammumma. She went into the house without glancing at me.

'It's murder. That's certain.'

'How many stab marks?' How that question took this shape I don't know, really.

'Stab? Not a drop of blood! That's the interesting thing.'

'Maybe a heart attack!'

'No, you come in here,' she said.

She called me into the kitchen and stood leaning by the hearth. I pulled out a wooden stool and sat on it. Amma served the story that she had heard on the way back piping hot. Apparently Soman Nair's wife, Subhadra, had an affair with two young men, and one day, when he came back home, he found them all naked and . . . at this point, Amma clapped her hand over her mouth and barely suppressed an 'Ayyo!' I knew what that Ayyo was about—she'd suddenly realized she was sharing this tale of adultery with her own son, and it had embarrassed her. I pretended not to notice all the expressions that rose and fell on her face, and got up from the wooden seat.

The autopsy report showed that Soman Nair had died of injury to his internal organs. Though no one knew who the murderer was, everyone privately suspected Subhadra's two lovers. But they all knew that they had actually left the place on the very night in which Soman Nair had caught them red-handed and butt-naked.

The police read the letters of apology that they had written to their wives. They were both working in a coffee plantation in Coorg now. The hottest topic of conversation, from dawn to dusk, in our parts, was about the identity of the killer. Since each one had a distinct story to tell, it was never boring.

I noticed not these stories but the fact that after Soman Nair's murder, Ammumma had revived her practice of going to the temple in the wee hours of dawn, something she had given up years back. And not only that, when she returned, she would shut herself up in her room for hours. No one could make out why. One day, when she was gone, I slipped into her room. With the same fear of years back, holding my breath, I shut the halves of the door. Now these halves were just two brittle planks in my hands. I searched the place generally to find out what she did for so many hours. I did not find anything especially new. Even after so many years, the key to the mundu box was still under her bed. I opened the box. In the diary that I found inside it, there were a lot of scrawled writing, in pencil and pen. Following that hand was difficult, but I soon realized it was a collection of the stories people around us were telling about Soman Nair's murder. In another notebook, she had noted some dates and times, and written a detailed account of the setting—of even how nature had been—before the murder. I tried hard to make sense of something she had inferred from measuring the gap between the times noted, but it was too hard.

One day, earlier than usual, around three in the morning, I woke up hearing something, and when I checked, I saw Ammumma gently close the door and go out of the house. I followed her. She was not even carrying a light. Probably because she was so used to walking on these village paths, she seemed utterly confident. I could not match her speed. She stopped when she reached the ridge on which the murder was committed. It was fifteen minutes past three then. She squatted near the place where the body was found, bent down, and seemed to be drawing in deep breaths. After a while, she pulled out a watch from her waist. I too looked at my watch: three-thirty now. According to the police, the murder was committed at exactly that time. My attention was hooked on to her. I shuddered inwardly, worried, wondering what she was going to do at this hour. Some moments passed, and then she started walking towards Subhadra's house. The little lane that led to that house was very narrow; only one person could walk on it at a time. If someone came the opposite way, you couldn't help brushing against them. And if you turned back suddenly, the person behind you had nowhere to hide. So I walked a bit behind her and then stopped there.

Ammumma came back before it was light. My parents knew nothing of it. I decided I was going to ask her a few things this time before I returned to work when my leave was over. It was the old fear that always held me back. Of course, there was no guarantee at all that I would receive a reply. Once before when I had asked, she had made some vague responses—that my grandfather had owned a printing press and that maybe the detective books she read came from there. What really worried me now was that she was actually after the murderer. With the keenness of a police dog. An aged woman! And besides, I began to suspect that there was tinge of happiness about her after this murder. If so, that was pretty unacceptable and unbearable. I made up my mind to ask, no matter what her retort might be. I did not bother to tell my parents any of this, either. Even today, our house is tied to the edge of her waist-cloth. No one says or does a thing beyond her look and gesture.

And so, one afternoon I went over to her room and knocked. She did not open the door. She came out only after two whole hours. By then, I was outside the house, helping my father to plant the banana saplings.

'Eda cherukka!' Acchan and I both shuddered at her call.

'Go,' Acchan said.

I felt strangely afraid. All the tales I had heard about her since my childhood rose up together and stood in front of me. Ammini Amma could summon anything that was lost . . . bring it back . . . she could see the dead . . . if the dark stood next to Ammini Amma, she could turn it to light . . .

I was now face to face with her. Amma was gesturing to me from behind—Don't ask her anything please.

'Eda, tell me, what is it that you want to know?'

I was speechless, frightened.

'Speak!'

I swallowed hard and asked: 'Who killed Soman Nair?'

Ammumma held me in a long stare and then turned and went inside. I heard her door shut. She came out from there only late in the night. I was sitting on the verandah then. She came and sat near me. 'Two days,' she said. 'I will tell you in two days.'

'I am going back tomorrow evening,' my voice trembled lightly.

'Never mind. I'll call you.' She got up.

The questions that had dried up inside my throat troubled me for some time.

The next morning, Mathai, who the ration shop owner, came running to the house, calling for my grandmother. Ammumma was standing in the front yard.

'They caught the murderer from Coimbatore! A Tamil fellow!'

I watched her. She was listening carefully to all that he said, betraying no emotion or any reaction. When Mathai left, I went up to her.

'So, the police caught him before you?'

Ammumma replied in a completely detached tone: 'He is not the killer.'

My heart suddenly felt all the more weighed down. I did not conceal it, and instead, in a single leap, asked, 'Then who?'

'Wait,' she said, 'and I will tell you.' She went back inside.

When I set off for Manipur, I just wanted the time to pass quickly. I reached home at midnight and told my wife all about the murder back home, how the police had caught the killer and how Ammumma had claimed that they were mistaken. Her face, naturally rosy, grew redder, I noticed. The pounding of the heart in suspense is just like solitude's contrivance to hunt alone. I could not bear it alone any more, so I had shared it with my wife. I felt better.

'Twenty-four hours more, right?' she asked.

'Yes,' I replied.

When twenty more hours passed, they called from home. My wife was standing beside me, listening in. She must have guessed it all from my replies on the phone. For some reason, I did not speak in her language but in Malayalam. Though she could not understand my Malayalam she made out that Ammumma had died. In her sleep. 'An easy death,' said Acchan.

After her cremation, when everyone had left, I stepped into her room without any fear. I went through her books and papers carefully. I felt the lightness of sitting in that room without feeling afraid. What really surprised me that day was the large collection of newspaper cuttings that I discovered in the room. It was under the bed, too. All of them were news stories about murders, of many kinds.

I did not wait for the funerary feast and the rituals. When I got back, my wife wanted to know who the real killer was. When she asked, I could see the strain of having stored up that question inside leaving her.

I had taken from the house only Ammumma's diary. I told her in detail all that she had written in it. When I saw the expression on her face grow more tense and drawn as I got past each page of the diary, I was forced to add things that Ammumma had not written. Before I reached the last page, I told her that the murderer was spotted on that page. My wife gulped down some water, looking rather pinched. When it seemed that the water had cooled her down somewhat, I told her, with my apologies, that someone had ripped off that page. Making an effort to prop up her heart which seemed be shrinking in disappointment she tried to smile but it was futile.

Originally published as
'Ammumma Detective' in 2018

Communist

Paacha

Turn left, get down from the Idappalli family's tapioca patch and you reach the fields owned by the Peedika family. Cross the ridge of the fields and you are in the yard of the Brahmin family, the Thekkedathu Mana. As he went through the yard full of nettles and weeds, Satan remembered the anjili tree that once looked like it was almost touching the sky. It used to be between two Puliyan mango trees. Remembering the golden yellow sweetness of the anijli fruit, Satan's mouth watered a little even at his age. In the hope that the anjili might feel a little love and grant a small fruit, he walked on looking for that place that had sunk roots in his memory. After he passed one or two coconut trees, he found a line of trees standing as though they were a row of soldiers, uniformed alike, without a shred of the dignity expected of trees. He opened his eyes a bit more and went over to find out who these new tree-fellows were. And when he came closer, he saw the milky white sap forming on their trunks, and these trees had no udders for sure . . . He came away shaking his head, saying now I know, now I know, to look where the anjili tree was, walking this and that way for some more time. The new-fangled fellows were all milky-sap-oozing rubber trees!

He kept walking by the edge of the yard on the rough path hewn by the feet of the people who went that way until he reached a narrow path to the left. The darkness had been walking with him all this way, so he did not know which direction to take. He waited, hoping to ask some passer-by. It was futile; no one came that way. Because age had dimmed his sight, his feet were not confident about walking in the dark. But soon, not wanting to keep waiting for long, he turned to the left. His feet hit the stones. He staggered; the thodali thorns on either side pricked and hurt his body.

A little way ahead, a burst of light appeared from somewhere and showed him the canal ahead, and the single-log bridge that lay across it. He was not brave enough to cross it on foot, so he knelt before it. He then sat on the log and slowly slid across it. When he reached the other side, the light parted ways with him. Darkness stood right in front of him unrelentingly. Two eyes descended from the ilavu tree near him.

'Saare, where are you going?'

His ears picked up the question that had tumbled into the dark. Where did this come from, they asked his eyes. His eyes went round and round, searching, while the two eyes sat on the bough above, shining.

'Who is that?' he threw the question back towards the bough.

'This is me, the only one who can see in the dark.'

'Oh, you, my dear child! I got sick of sitting at home and came out for a walk. It got dark, and I can't see the way back too well.'

'Ayyo, but your house is to the west, saar!'

Satan's eyes and legs started moaning, ayyo, we can't, we can't, *vayye, vayye* . . . and he said, 'My child, I don't think I can walk that far.'

'What to do then?'

His legs and arms and eyes asked each other.

'Hope it's all right to ask, tell me if there's a house you know where they'll let me stay for the night. I'll be off at the first sight of dawn.'

It hopped from branch to branch up there thinking about finding a place in the dead of the night. Then said, 'There's one place . . . but will it be . . . all right?'

'I'm okay anywhere, child.'

'A priest lives there.'

'Why not? I am fine with that.'

'Okay, then let's go.'

'Child, fly a bit slow. I am not as fast as I used to be.'

This is a clump of screw-pine, look, this is the bank of a pond, the frogs are going krom-krom-krom from those fields—as he flew ahead, the owl sifted the sights he could gather from above and presented them to Satan. Grasping the thread of the owl's screech, Satan walked behind.

'I'll come only till the doorstep. That's all right, I hope?'

'If it is dark still, how will I go in, child?'

'The light from the church falls on the priest's doorstep too.'

'That will do.'

The church was a small tiled one with walls from which the plaster was falling off, with a cemetery for just a few. There was a small house beside it, as old as the church.

'Look, that's the house.'

Like the owl had mentioned, the light from the church was all over its roof and front yard.

'I am grateful, child,' said Satan.

When he stepped into the yard of the parish priest's house, the light woke up, took a look and then turned over again. As he walked softly so as not to hurt the light, Satan wondered if the priest would get frightened at the sight of an unfamiliar being so late, in the dark. But when he asked himself why the priest, who lived by the fear of God, should be afraid of him, the doubt disappeared. Then another doubt came running. What should he say if the priest asked his name? Gods have thirty-three crores of names. But what about him? Maybe he could reduce his present name to, say, 'Satyan' or 'Sam'. But that would be wrong, wouldn't it? He had never lied in all these long years. To lie at this late stage in life, that too to a priest, would be so wrong. *It's better to spit out the truth if asked.*

When he rang the bronze bell gently, the priest's voice, wheezy with age, came up gently and beckoned him in.

'The door is not bolted. Come right in.'

The door opened. The priest was having supper. A chicken leg was declaring to him: I oppose you. Blaspheming God? The priest asked it in all seriousness.

Kid goats can admit defeat to priests; so can altar boys and the sexton; so also a fowl while it is still alive. But if a piece of meat were to become so defiant as to raise the question why it should admit defeat again after it had been turned into somebody's food, then that was the ultimate assertion of freedom, thought Satan. But since that was not the moment to state this thought openly, he merely knocked.

'Come in quick and have some dinner,' said the priest. 'It's already quite late. Have to be out soonest.'

He was still in contest with the chicken leg; he had not raised his face to look. His teeth were losing their battle. As Satan continued to stand at the doorstep wondering why he still fought so furiously, knowing fully well what the Final Judgment was, the priest flung the chicken leg down at the edge of his plate with a fury that matched that of the heavens condemning a sinner to the depths of hell. The priest, however, hid the face of the defeated man, and looked up towards the door.

A face so tired that it looked like it was ready to fall asleep the instant it spied a bed; legs so worn that they seemed to be seeking some warm water to soak the weary feet.

'Come in quick,' he repeated as he rose to wash his hands. 'Have some supper. We have to leave soon after.'

The priest had probably mistaken him for someone else. Why else would he speak thus to a stranger visiting him so late? He was about to ask when the priest said from where he was washing his hands: 'I knew that you would come. Please don't just stand there. Please come in.'

Satan had heard that some priests possessed a divine eye. He entered the house marvelling at that ability of the priest at his advanced age—the divine eye never succumbs to cataract, his own eyes told him.

As he approached the table greedily, his hand began to murmur: 'Hey, I stink of that coconut tree trunk you were clinging on. Save me from it.' The water baptized them and the coconut tree stink was swept away, giving way to the scent of soap. Satan's hands came together to give thanks to that scent. The soap was filled with wonder. Not a single one among those who rubbed all their dirt on it and took away its soul in return had ever bothered to give thanks! They never cared to cast a compassionate look on that body, which wasted and grew thinner each time the dirt was rubbed on it. Here were two hands now, clasped together in gratitude! The soap cast her perfume-laden smile on them.

'There's excellent beef and chicken curry,' said the priest, pushing the bowls towards Satan.

'Ayyo, I won't eat any of it,' he said.

'The beef is as smooth as butter. But the chicken— he's a bit tough. But that's the thing about country chicken!' The priest threw a vexed look at the curry.

'Not, not that . . . I am a vegetarian.'

'Ayyo, here we have only some warmed buttermilk— *moru* curry—and pickles!' The priest sounded apologetic.

So the priest's divine eye cannot divine the guest's culinary preferences, thought Satan, as he poured the moru-curry into the rice, mixed it into rice-balls, which he proceeded to eat.

When the priest left the supper table to go into another room, Satan peered into the priest's room. On the wall were images of Lord Jesus, the Virgin Mother, Father St Chavara, St Alphonsa and a calendar from the *Deepika* newspaper. In the room beyond this one was a cot, some clothes, a Bible resting on the pillow and a long torch.

'Finished?' asked the priest who had now returned with a muffler around his neck.

'Yes, almost.' Satan got up, picking up his plate after licking his fingers well.

The priest closed the windows and said a prayer before the icon. He crossed himself.

'Okay, let us go now,' he said, and turning to Satan, added, 'I know that you are very tired.'

'Never mind, Father,' replied Satan.

The priest locked the door and stepped out of the house.

He switched on the torch and a powerful beam leapt like a kangaroo to reach the neighbours' grounds. Before they were out of the churchyard, the priest began to chat with Satan.

'How old are you now?'

Satan had not expected this rather puzzling question at this moment. When he realized that he would be as confused if Satan asked in return how old God was, the priest proceeded to answer his own question.

'You are older than me—your face shows.'

Satan nodded. He was ahead, so the priest did not notice.

'Older people are riper, more mature. Also, when someone like you is with me, I become more confident.'

Satan did not really understand what he meant. Not because he was old and senile, but because it sounded like a signal-phrase that preceded a secret. Humans do this all the time—say something and then hide many other things inside it. Is 'human' a name so great?

His legs were not bothered by such mysteries. They, of course, had no need to be bothered thus, either. Where was the priest taking them? Was it far? Was the way there full of mud and stones? Each step was steeped in such concerns.

Suddenly, the priest said: 'Have to give the final sacraments to someone. Not far now.'

Satan's legs froze at this.

The priest switched the torch off for a moment and turned it on again.

'Is it difficult to walk?' he asked.

'No,' replied Satan's legs from where they stood.

Who was awaiting death this night? As Satan followed the priest thinking why the family of such a person could not arrange for a vehicle so that the elderly priest did not have to find his way in the dark, the latter said, 'The man awaiting death is my older brother.'

The light from his torch staggered and lurched a bit, touching and falling on both sides of the way through which they were walking. Satan did not reply.

The light carried the two old men through paths on which the sounds of the night had entwined themselves. They reached a garden of rubber trees.

The tiny insects from the rubber trees came and sat on the priest's brown-coloured habit. Some walked up and down it. Some were unmoving.

'Let's go this way. Not through the front of the house.'

The light cleaved the darkness inside the garden of rubber trees in two. As they covered the distance between the garden and his older brother's house, the priest sliced the history of his family neatly as though he had measured that distance:

'I have no memory of seeing this chettayi of mine. He left our house when I was five and joined the communist party. My father wanted to educate him and make him a priest. When he left the house and became a communist, no one would marry our sisters. My mother stopped talking altogether. I joined the seminary because my father wished me to. That year, our father hung himself to death. I've heard that Chettayi spent his days in Kolkata and Andhra, somewhere . . . He's been back two years now. We haven't met. I've heard that he lives alone. Had heard that he was unwell since some days now. Anything may happen to him now, any time . . .'

A small yard opened out where the garden ended. It ended behind an unplastered house. The priest pushed open the back door. It opened without any protest. He stepped in first.

'Come,' he called.

A man lay in the room where a dim light hung back, wheezing hard. The priest stood silent, gazing at his face for a long while.

Satan looked around. Bottles of medicines, books, a half-empty bottle of rum.

Peering at a photo stuck on the wall behind the cot, the priest said, 'That's our father, I think.'

Satan noticed even in the dark that the photo was of a Chinese man, but he did not correct the priest, leaning on the principle that the priest's belief should hold him up.

After some time, the priest asked if it was possible to suck out the light in the room. Satan did it for him.

The priest's prayer could not be heard in the darkness. Maybe the poor man was weeping within himself for his misguided brother. Maybe he was kissing his face. Maybe he was violating the rules of the Church, and they were getting to know each other as siblings who shared the deep tie of blood, beyond being a priest and a communist.

As he stood quietly in the dark, Satan suddenly felt the stab of tears in his eyes as he remembered his life of loneliness with no one by his side even in this ripe old age. He held them back and leaned on the wall; gradually the sounds eddying in the dark began to recede. When the room had sunk into total silence, Satan heard the priest say, 'Let there be only darkness now.'

That small spark of light re-entered the room now.

'All right, let us leave?' the priest asked.

Satan, his face drawn and scared, looked at the priest who was now coming away from the cot.

Not letting his eyes fall on the look on Satan's face, rubbing off the breath that he had pulled out under the cover of darkness, the priest switched on the long beam of light and stepped out into the open.

Originally published as
'Kammunist Paccha' in 2018

Dirt
Road

When they saw the police jeep jump from stone to stone on the dirt road, the local people had no doubt. It was going to Mesthiri's house. It was always like that. The jeep skipped and jumped like it was playing hopscotch and stopped in front of Mesthiri's house, sounding pretty washed out. Two policemen leapt out from the back before the sub-inspector could step out. The older one of the two threw open the gate and walked briskly towards the house. There was some distance to walk. The weeds and grass from the yard had made their way into the walking path. Before he reached the house, the policeman called aloud to Mesthiri. Vava, who was standing behind the house with his feet drenched in piss after a failed attempt to reach the guava tree with the jet, recognized the voice to be that of the police constable Narayanan. He rubbed his feet together to get rid of the wetness, wiped the last drop of urine with the edge of his lungi and ran to the front of the house.

'Where is Mesthiri, eda?' asked Narayanan.

Vava answered, looking at the new SI who was walking up from behind Narayanan. 'He's inside. Lying down.'

The policeman gestured with his eyes to call him.

'Please sit here, saar,' Vava said, wiping the dust off the verandah.

'I'll tell you when we come to stay,' said the policeman. 'Go. Get him now.'

Vava lingered a second, reluctant, and then asked if the head constable could spare a minute in private. Narayanan went with him to a corner.

'Who's this fellow?' asked the SI to the other policeman.

'One of Mesthiri's minions. Real name is Ashraf; he is called Vava.'

Narayanan heard Vava out and told him, 'Eda, this is a new officer. If you fuck things up, I am going to dump you.'

'For heaven's sake, it is the truth, saar,' Vava bowed his head.

Narayanan hummed firmly and strode up to the SI. Vava followed him. Noticing that the SI's gaze was falling on his naked torso pitilessly, he tried to cover it with the towel on his shoulder, but the mathematical signs etched by the sword-stick and the knife still showed.

'Saare,' Narayanan took off his cap, scratching his head mildly. 'This guy says that he's in bed, shitting blood, apparently. Why not go inside . . .'

The SI drew a deep breath, wiped his shoes hard on the doormat and stepped on to the verandah. Vava, who had leapt on to the verandah too, pushed opened the door of the house and ran into Mesthiri's room.

He called out to Mesthiri, who was all wrapped up inside a large woollen blanket: 'Mesthiri, please get up . . .'

Vava's voice did not penetrate that tortoise-shell of a heavy blanket. He called again; Mesthiri did not hear him.

'Louder!' said the head constable who now came in banging loudly on the frame on the door. At this, the form that was swathed in the woollen blanket stirred somewhat.

'Mesthiriye, leave your sanctum for the moment, come out. Some of us have come to visit you,' Narayanan bent down and whispered.

Vava brought a chair from another room for the SI. Sitting down, he asked Narayanan, 'That's your guy, right? Why? Didn't he hear you?'

Narayanan forced a smile.

'So we have to wait till His Highness opens his royal eyelids?' the SI asked the policemen.

'Mesthiri, wake up! The saars have come to see you,' whispered Vava into his ears, kneeling by the side of the bed. He did not hear him.

'Get up, you son of a bitch,' roared the SI, still seated, kicking the side of the bed really hard. Constable Mathen pulled the blanket off Mesthiri's face. The SI threw his cruelest look at him, but his eyes were still shut.

'Saare,' Mesthiri said very slowly. 'The pain's unbearable, that's why I am not opening my eyes. It was bleeding all of last night. Haven't slept for four or five days now because of it. Just tell me why you are here, saars?'

The policemen and the SI looked at each other. Narayanan caught what the SI was hinting at.

'Where were you last night?'

'Narayanan, saare, in the past four days I haven't been out of this room and the toilet.'

'Were you at the Karippoothattu toddy shop yesterday?'

'It's been long time since I stopped going to such places, saare. It's all adulterated, Palakkadan toddy. You'll shit your ass out. You tell me why you are here, saar.'

'Tell me, who busted Vadakkan's ass last night?'

Mesthiri's eyes opened languidly, like a flower blooming. Staring at the blades of the dust-covered fan above, he lay still for a few minutes and asked, 'Who? Our Sabu?'

In reply to the hmm that came as an answer, he turned his head and said, 'Ah! Mathen saar! You have come too!'

Mathen did not smile; he tried to maintain a grim look.

'Did Sabu tell you that I did it?'

'Does he have to say that you did it?'

Turning his eyes towards that unfamiliar voice, Mesthiri seemed reluctant to withdraw his gaze. 'The new SI, right?'

No one replied.

'He's handsome.' Mesthiri looked at the new SI with a mild smile.

The SI felt unsettled for a moment. The policemen pretended not to hear.

'Saare, he knows that I won't snare him. It's been two years since Sabu and I split the turf. We, however, fish only for what fills our nets. We won't use snare nets against each other—that's our word to each other!'

'Then who scraped out his butt?' The SI pulled his chair closer. 'Bloody stinking fur on your crotch! Just spit it out easy, ok? Or you'll spit out the blood you are shitting right now.'

'My saare, not me! My word is good as gold. If you want to make sure, just ask them.'

The SI looked at the two policemen. They did not utter a word.

'Then who did that special surgery on your behalf?' asked the SI.

Mesthiri looked at Narayanan puzzled, clearly not getting it.

'Someone poked a sword-stick in Sabu's anus and twisted it. That's Mesthiri's style, isn't it? Saar got to know. That's why he's asking.'

'My saare, some bastard's trying to frame me. Believe me.'

The SI was silent for some more moments.

'Or, if you want me to come with you, I will. But I am not the culprit.'

'He's in the ICU now. We'll take his statement once he is conscious.' The SI turned towards Vava. 'If it's your Mesthiri's name that he gives, then make sure you bring a thicker blanket so that you can scoop up anything that's left.'

Vava nodded.

Before the SI stepped out of the room, Mesthiri called, 'Saare.'

He turned. Mesthiri turned his neck towards him and said: 'There's a chap from Mahe, Vella. I was waiting for him. A small keyhole surgery.' He straightened his neck and closed his eyes gently: 'If the work is being done in your station's limits, no need to come here. I'll come over there.'

The SI and the policemen went out of the house. Vava went with them till the gate. Narayanan and Mathen, who were sitting at the back in the jeep, did not look at them. When the jeep began to skip over the stones, Narayanan threw a sidelong glance to see if Vava was still standing by the doorway.

'Did you make the usual, uh, the sacred offering? Prasaadam?'

'The SI's new . . . he might . . .' Vava sounded doubtful.

'The new one will try to lick clean even the roof! Just give it to Narayanan.'

Vava nodded.

Hearing someone call him Chetaa, Vava went out. The child who delivered the milk stood there. He took the bottle of milk from her, and, noticing a young woman of twenty or twenty-three standing behind her, asked: 'Who's this?'

The child turned around to look. She noticed the woman behind her only then. She shrugged her shoulders to say she did not know.

'Who are you, girl?'

'I am here to see Mesthiri.'

'Off you go! This is no place for women.'

'But then what about this girl and that woman cutting the grass?'

'Are you like this tiny kid and that old hag past seventy?' Vava leapt down from the verandah angrily, but the child said, 'Chetaa, please take the milk and give me the bottle? I have to go to school!'

'What's your name, child?'

'Rosamma. What's yours, chechi?'

'Padmini.'

'Who gave you such a big name? A real big one!'

'My school name is Andrea V. Samuel. I don't like it—it's a *challu* name, bad!' Padmini laughed.

Vava came back wearing a checked shirt and handed over the empty bottle to Rosamma. She took it and left.

'Edi, girl, you go someplace that suits you. This is a different sort of location.'

'After seeing . . . Mesthiri?'

'Didn't I tell you it won't work?'

'Just one thing . . . I have to tell him just one thing.'

'I told you, it won't work,' he hollered; it scared her.

'Who's out there?' Mesthiri's tired voice came out of the house.

'No one.'

Vava came close to her, and Padmini felt that her body was being blessed by the stink of stale toddy.

'Do you want to return in one piece? Or without your nose and breast?'

Padmini did not feel afraid; she felt nauseous. She ran back to the gate, pressed her hands on it and bent down. A few guttural noises escaped her, and a few long strands of phlegm and saliva came loose from her throat.

Vava went back in. Mesthiri had called him. He reached Mesthiri's room before his voice reached him.

'Change this bloodstained cloth.'

When he held Mesthiri's hand to help him up, he pushed it away and stood up on his own. He walked up and down the room a few times and stood still again.

'How are things?'

'Pappan is in Mahe now. A radar's been set up by Cheeran and Kandippokkar at Koduvalli.'

'When will we know?'

'Before noon.'

Mesthiri went to the toilet. He squatted. His right hand rested on his right knee. In the Chinmaya mudra of the thumb and forefinger he held a lit bidi that Vava had made for him, and the thick swirls of smoke from it climbed up the wall with an unsteady gait.

Cheeran turned up before noon. Mesthiri was lying in bed, on his stomach. When he entered the room, Mesthiri said, 'There's no time now.'

'I know.'

'When?'

'Tonight, Vella's coming to meet Thommikkunhu.'

'What about the lad?'

'That . . .'

'Tell me about the lad!' Mesthiri said.

'They're planning to take him.'

'Take him where?'

'To Dubai, I heard.'

'Where did you hear this?'

'Kandippokkar told me.'

Mesthiri did not speak for some time. He pressed his face on the pillow.

'So Vella's dealings with Thommikkunhu are direct?'

'Yes,' said Cheeran. 'Tonight he'll be entrusted with the gold for the Swami and the Brahmin. They wanted us to hand over their stuff to him.'

'When's the ritual?'

'Past one. It's at the Meditation Centre owned by Thommikunhu's brother-in-law, near the highway.'

Mesthiri hummed.

'Where's my boy now?'

'Couldn't mark him. Pokker's keeping a watch.'

Mesthiri called Vava. Vava gave him a bidi. Before going to the toilet he said. 'I am going to drill a hole the size of this thumb. And then I'll push in this copper ring, just to make it look pretty.'

Vava and Cheeran nodded. The door of the toilet shut.

The gold for the jewellery shop at Thekkekkaattu came through the fellow from Mahi, Vella. The gold to the southern parts would reach Swami in Alappuzha. Swami divided it among the Brahmins in Thrissur and the Syrian Christians in Kottayam. When his people got caught in the Nedumbassery and Karipur airports, he stepped back into the Green Room. Mesthiri's good times began when Vella agreed to supply gold if trustworthy and hardy men could be dispatched. It was Kandippokkar who introduced Mesthiri, who was lazing around, gambling and getting into petty fights, to Swami. Kandippokkar was a pimp who supplied boys, fresh as juicy green gourds. He was Mesthiri's old chum. He also supplied Swami with kids. He introduced Mesthiri when Swami asked him if he could find grown men and not children. Mesthiri delivered the stuff and not even the rain or wind knew. Whenever Swami handed over the sum demanded with no questions asked, Mesthiri's eyes were always on the boy who was with Swami.

'Leave it, Saami didn't hand him over even though Vella was eyeing him!'

'Just get him for me, Pokkare,' Mesthiri would beg him.

'Saami won't give him.'

'But why?'

'That boy's so special, real special right?'

'You give the best chaps only to high-caste people?'

'What are you saying! Saami swooped in on him the moment he came!'

When they began to catch the smugglers at Nedumbassery and Karipur and Bombay, the flow of gold became a trickle. Swami, the Brahmin and gold jewellery shop owners met Vella. Vella had a single demand. He drew Swami aside and let him know. When Swami stayed silent, Vella said, 'Give me the gold you have, I'll get it to the shore even if I have to use a local dhow.'

Before he handed over the boy to Kandippokkar, Swami left a love-bite on his tender nipple. Pokker's vehicle left Swami's house and then stopped once. Mesthiri did not get out. Vava and Paappan brought the boy. Pokker stood on the other side of the car window and said, 'Mesthiri, this is a fraud sale.'

'The pleasure's in it, isn't it?'

'Vella's going to come searching.'

'Tell him that this gold's been gifted to me.'

At night, Swami's people came looking for Mesthiri. They couldn't find him. Vella's people came too. They too failed to find him.

Mesthiri took the boy and went on a tour of Ooty and Kodaikanal. Then they came to Coorg and to Wayanad. When they were staying in a hotel in Coorg, the boy ran his fingers through Mesthiri's hair and beard and said, 'Shave this off, it bites!'

'If you tell me I'll cut off my neck,' said Mesthiri. He got ready to go to the barber shop at once.

Mesthiri told the boy not to open the door for anyone. He agreed.

'I'll slip in this coin under the door. Open only then.'

He said yes.

When he got out of the hotel, suddenly Mesthiri ran back to the room and knocked on the door. It did not open. When he slipped the coin under the door, the boy opened the door. Mesthiri embraced him and kissed him firmly on his lips. 'Lock the door and stay there,' he told him; the boy did.

When Mesthiri went out again, a single coin was slid under the door again. It let out a scraping sound on the smooth floor. The boy opened the door.

When Mesthiri returned, the scent of attar still lingered in the room.

The juddering and jerking on the road made Mesthiri's bum ache. Cheeran was driving as carefully as he could, but the stones that jutted out in the twists and turns of the road kept cheating him. Each time it happened it was as if the heat and agonizing pain inside Mesthiri's ass was going to rent it apart. He was a little bit relieved when they got on to the highway, leaving behind the dirt road.

'Which district is Vella touring now?' he asked.

'Pappan's following him. He left Chalakkudy a little while ago, he said.'

'Mm-hmm,' Mesthiri reacted.

Cheeran stopped the vehicle in front of Thommikunhu's brother-in-law's Meditation Centre. All three of them got out. They leapt over the wall, crouched in the dark and waited.

After some time, Pappan called. He said that Vella's car had turned off the highway.

'Have they changed the location?' Vava felt unsure.

'Let's wait,' said Mesthiri.

They waited till dawn. No one came.

When they were returning, Mesthiri asked Cheeran. 'How is Vella's driver Kabir?'

'Let's see,' Cheeran replied.

The light that elongated into the front yard had gone up and touched Vava's weenie, which lay quiet, like a smaller sleep ensconced within a larger slumber. Vava lay flat on his back on the veranda, snoring, with his mundu flung apart, exposing his legs and the sleeping weenie between them. Padmini, who had climbed on to the veranda noiselessly, heard someone sing from inside in a raspy voice—but its pitch and tempo were both correct. It was a popular Malayalam song, one that she knew:

> *Oh young virginal one,*
> *Oh Prince, who*
> *makes it rain honey*
> *in the pavilion of jaggery-laden sweetness . . .*
> *Chakkarappandalil . . .*

Padmini peered at the direction from which the song flowed. It was from the east room. The same lines were repeated again and again. It always felt as if the song would flow into the next line this time for sure, but it kept going right back to the line about the young and virginal prince. Bored of hearing the same lines, Padmini stepped into the next line:

The desire I have to come and be
the Princess of the land of your dreams . . .

The flow of the song from inside the room stopped suddenly.

'Who?' a deep voice asked.

'It is I. I came here yesterday.'

No reply came from the other side.

'Vave!' the voice roared. Padmini was terrified.

'Don't call him. I'll go away.'

Before going away, Padmini went close to the window, pressed against it and said, 'Mesthiri, let me tell you something, please don't be angry.'

She waited for a few moments, and when there was no reply, said:

'The lyrics of the song . . . It is not *chakkarappandal*, it is *sarkarappandal* . . .'

For a moment, Mesthiri was completely stunned. This was a song he had sung full-throated as long as he could remember—with friends, in the toddy shop, on wedding-eves, in the bathroom every day. He had heard this song, from a popular Malayalam play, for the first time on the maidan near his father's house at

Pandalam, as a child. He had been singing it since then and people always enjoyed it, but not a single person had corrected his lyrics. He had been kicked in the navel by the police, some had stabbed him from the back—the pain then had been trivial, and he had shaken it off. But this felt enormously shameful. Mesthiri felt that the blood dripping in his toilet was falling from his heart.

When Padmini left as silently as she had come, Vava was still asleep spreadeagled like before. When she had gone some way she heard the roar again: 'Vave!' She walked as fast as she could, despairing that the way seemed endless, when Vava appeared on a bike and barred her way.

Vava went in and returned after some time.

'Come in.'

Padmini left her slippers outside and went in.

As she went along the corridors of the house, fear sucked off the moisture from her throat.

'Mesthiri . . .' Vava called.

Mesthiri was sitting on his cot. He turned his head sharply, and saw the frail girl standing behind Vava.

'Come in,' he said.

Padmini stepped in.

'Sit.'

She sat down.

'Why did you come yesterday and today?'

'To meet you, Mesthiri?'

'And?'

'I need a job.'

'Hey wench, there aren't any jobs here that you can do.' It was Vava who replied.

'I'll be happy with the work that you do.'

Vava looked at Mesthiri.

'What is that?' Mesthiri asked her.

'The goonda's job.'

Mesthiri lit a bidi. He held it in between his ring finger and small finger, closed his other fingers to form a small well, pressed his lips on it and took a deep puff.

'Are you studying?' he asked.

Padmini nodded.

'What?'

'Engineering.'

'Then can't you just be an engineer?'

'But don't I have to pass the exams? Too many supplementary exams . . . won't pass.'

'Then why the hell did you drag yourself there?'

'Who dragged who? My father and mother dragged me there! I wanted to study music. They sent me to the engineering college saying that my uncle, my father's younger brother, had destroyed his life with the singing and concerts and all . . .'

'Vave, get us two teas,' Mesthiri said.

Vava went into the kitchen.

'Who sent you to me?

'No one. There's a fellow in my class, Benny, who's a big fan of yours. He's the one who told us stories about you—how you turn off the main switch and climb on top of the transformer at night, how you chopped off someone neck jumping on him from the top of a coconut tree . . . I'd decided then that I want to be here. Had to search a bit to find this place. When I came yesterday, that chetan here shooed me off saying that women are not allowed here . . . I took a chance and came once again.'

Vava brought the tea.

'Have you eaten anything, girl?'

'No.'

'Drink the tea first,' he said, and turning to Vava, he asked him to get her something to eat from Aniyan Pillai's teashop.

'But they will have only appams and egg curry now.'

'Just get what they have. Get it for me only if its duck eggs.'

Vava nodded.

'You'll get hurt in our line of work.'

'I know.'

'It'll be full of police and case and mess.'

'Never mind. Let the family stink a bit.'

Mesthiri stubbed the bidi against the leg of the cot and threw it out of the window.

'Isn't it better to become a singer? You sing well, girl.'

'You sing well too, Mesthiri? Why didn't you become a singer?'

He chuckled aloud at that. The sound of Vava's bike fell on it.

'Drink your tea. It will get cold,' said Mesthiri, sipping his own tea.

Padmini picked up the cup and began to blow into it.

'Okay, let me ask you something,' asked Mesthiri with much reluctance.

'What?'

'That is . . .' His reluctance refused to budge.

'Tell me straight, Mesthiri!'

'Is it . . . really *sarkkarapandal*?

'What? Tell me, Mesthiri.'

'No . . . didn't you say . . . about the song . . .'

'Yes, yes. I swear on my mother. My uncle said so.'

'Are you sure?'

'Very sure.'

Mesthiri hummed *sarkkarapandalil* . . . in his mind. But it still came out 'cha'-first. He hummed inwardly for some more time and sang '*Sarkkarapandalil* . . .'

'Mesthiri, your song is *kidu*! Just great!' said Padmini, listening closely.

A shy smile spread on his face. The sound of Vava's bike rushed noisily into the front yard.

Vava ran inside, 'Vadakkan Sabu's kicked the bucket!'

213

Mesthiri put the teacup down.

'Did they get his statement?'

'Yes.'

'Whose name did he say?'

'I don't know. Should we move off somewhere?' Vava asked.

'He won't let us down, Vave. He is a Vadakkan—from the north—only by name. He's a first-rate southie, you can trust him!'

'But still?'

Mesthiri looked at Padmini. 'Girl, you can go.'

'But will you let me join you?'

Mesthiri turned to Vava. 'Get her an autorickshaw.'

Mesthiri never thought of the dead. Even if he did, he never kept them in his mind for long. But Sabu stayed there for a while longer than usual. And then went away.

When Mesthiri squatted on the closet, the glottis of his piles thrust itself out of its den and let down its tongue of blood on to the closet's whiteness. He had not slept since the boy vanished. If he so much as dozed, the copper-coloured thickets sprouting below the boy's waist would appear before his eyes. When his tongue would swim up his thighs, Mesthiri's dark-skinned dick would spring alert like a monkey ready to leap. He would split open his red lips to take Mesthiri's darkness into the pool of saliva inside. It would swim in there touching both walls of cheeks. When it seemed that the boy would rise higher

than a wave through his memory and emerge into the
open splitting his head apart, Mesthiri shut his eyes tight
and drowned the memory. The stream of blood flowed
down, moistening both banks in his anus.

'Mesthiri . . .' Cheeran was outside the toilet.

The response was a grunt, from all the straining to
poop.

'Vella is back from Koduvalli. He will see
Thommukunhu. In the evening he will fly out from
Nedumbassery with the boy.'

'It won't be a useless wait like last night?'

'No. The informer is Kabir.'

'Vella's driver?'

'Yes.'

'What's his demand?'

'Three-fourths of the gold he's bringing.'

'Don't make it three-fourths. If he'll bring back my
golden boy, the gold can be all his.'

Mesthiri cleaned himself up and came out, wiping
his face with the edge of his mundu. He threw a look
at Vava and Cheeran. Knowing what that meant, Vava
handed him the sword-stick.

'It'll be a disgrace to put just plain iron into Vella's
butt. He's a big aristocrat, isn't he? Let's add some
mercury in the hole.'

Testing its sharpness by brushing his finger on it,
Mesthiri handed it back to Vava.

After they left, he took a bath. Streaked his forehead with sandalwood paste. Opened the windows. Sat down and closed his eyes. He opened them when he heard someone calling his name.

'May I come in?'

'Come in,' said Mesthiri.

Padmini entered. Seeing Mesthiri fresh from his bath with sandalwood paste on his forehead, she was amazed. She stood quietly, savouring that sight for a few moments and then took out a bunch of bananas from her bag.

'Excellent kadali bananas,' she said. 'My roommate is from Konni. This is from her home garden.'

Mesthiri looked at the bananas.

'Eat! This was my breakfast today.'

Seeing that he did not move, Padmini pulled out one from the bunch humming the song about the crow sitting on the kadali-banana tree and held it out to him. 'Eat it, Mesthiri.'

'Do you know which movie this song is in?'

'No, no idea,' said Padmini.

'*Umma*. Lyrics by P. Bhaskaran, music by Baburaj. It was sung by Jikki.'

'Jikki?' The name amused Padmini. 'Is there such a name?'

'Of course, and she was a terrific singer,' said Mesthiri, and recollecting something, he sang the song

'Manjaadikkili myna, Mailanjikkili myna . . .' Padmini had not heard it before.

'That is a cool song,' she said.

'This Jikki is A.M. Raja's wife.'

Padmini was hearing that name for the first time too.

'Have you heard Raja's "Akashagangayude Karayil . . ."'

'No, never.'

Her reply left him somewhat displeased.

Mesthiri got up from the cot and went over to a corner of the room to open a wooden box.

'Come here, girl,' he called to her. 'I'll show you some of my old weapons.'

Padmini jumped up eagerly and went to him. In the small darkness inside the box she saw old cinema notices, song books of old movies.

'Look, see this?' Mesthiri picked out an old notice carefully. 'This was the notice of *Neelakkuyil*.'

Padmini touched *Neelakkuyil*.

'I got it from my neighbour Vasu who lived in the south-side house for five peanuts and ten paise!'

Padmini took a notebook from inside the box and opened it. It was full of writings in Tamil.

'What's this?'

'Songs of Saundarrajan and Sheerkazhi,' he said.

'Who wrote it?'

'Me, who else? To get a chance to sing in Tamil movies, you have to read Tamil, right? So I studied Tamil too.'

'And why did you not sing?'

The reply was Saundarrajan's 'Paattum naane . . .' and a guffaw.

'Can I ask you something please?'

'Girl, I know what you are going to ask. I won't reply, so don't bother.'

Padmini did not say anything for some time.

'Girl, your voice is the same as our old Jensi's.'

'Which Jensi?'

'There used to be a Jensi in the Cochin Chorus. Used to sing Ilayaraja's songs. How she used to sing!'

'Really?'

'Haven't you heard songs like "Kaathal Oviyum . . . "?'

'No.'

'Then what the fuck have you heard?' Mesthiri was irked. 'Don't know A.M. Raja, don't know Jikki!'

'But I am only twenty-three!'

'Do the ten-year-old kids sing Thyagaraja compositions because they are one hundred and fifty years old?'

'Are cinema songs like that? I just know a few cinema songs. Other than that . . .'

'If you love music, you must hear it all, learn it all, don't go around treating it like the stuff in your loin-cloth!'

'But why are you being so rude to me for that?'

'So, what should I do? Recite shlokas?'

'But I am not a singer.'

'Then?'

'I loved music, but it didn't work out, so I let it go.'

'Girl, if you let something you love go, even God cannot help you get it back.'

'Why is that?'

'It's like that!'

'I don't want it back. I left it.'

Mesthiri was silent for a while. Then he lit another bidi and asked, 'Are you sure?'

Padmini nodded—yes.

The car took the cut on the left of Bund Road and went downhill. Padmini asked, 'Where are we going?'

Mesthiri did not answer. The car ran on for some time and then stopped.

'Pappa, where are Vava and Cheeran?'

'In the engine room,' Pappan said, coming over after locking the car.

As they walked on, Padmini asked again: 'Where are we going?'

Mesthiri was still silent. They walked through a coconut garden and climbed on to a ridge. Pappan ran ahead. Before they reached the engine room, Vava came out of it.

'The boy?'

'He's safe. With Kandippokkar.'

'His passport?'

'Burned it.'

'Give Kabir the full amount,' said Mesthiri and stepped into the room. The scent of the attar from that room in Wayanad appeared first as he went in.

Seeing Vella gagged, Mesthiri asked, 'What is this for?'

'Oh, he trumpets too much,' Vava said.

'Pull off his mundu and briefs and get him to bend down.'

Pappan pulled off his clothes. Cheeran landed a blow behind his neck and got him to bow and bend.

Vava handed the sword-stick to Mesthiri.

Mesthiri turned around to look and asked, 'There was another one with us?'

Vava went out of the engine room. He told Padmini, who was toying nervously with the coconut-frond thatch of its roof, that Mesthiri was asking for her.

When he heard her footsteps, he said, 'Come up here, girl.'

Padmini went up there. He held out the sword-stick to her. She did not take it, and looked utterly terrified.

'This is my kadali banana. C'mon, take it!'

Padmini was about to burst into tears.

When he roared 'Take it, edi!' she took it tearfully. Seeing her hand and the weapon shake feverishly, he snapped, 'Stop shivering!'

Padmini agreed, weeping.

'Girl,' Mesthiri called.

She saw his image through a cloak of tears—it seemed vague and swimming fuzzily.

'Plunge that sharp thing you're holding straight into that bent guy's ass and pull it out.'

Padmini squealed fearfully; Mesthiri snarled at her to stop. The thatched engine room shook in his fury. Padmini was petrified. She swallowed her tears.

'It's okay to miss the first time. It happens. Gradually your aim will improve.'

Mesthiri sat down on the iron stool.

Padmini went over and stood behind Vella, trembling.

'Velle, it's a girl who doesn't know the place well. Open your legs a bit, uh?' Mesthiri said.

Vella did not hear him. When Vava lifted a leg and aimed at Vella's loins, Mesthiri said, 'Don't ruin his balls. He'll open.'

Vella opened his legs.

'Pappa, show the girl where to nail the stump?'

Pappan opened Vella's buttocks. Padmini turned her head away sharply.

'Look carefully, girl,' said Mesthiri. 'If your eyes fail you, everything else fails.'

Padmini did not dare to look.

'Look,' said Mesthiri again, his voice cool and serene. That made Padmini all the more fearful. She looked.

'There, right there—just push it in slowly.'

Padmini's breath began to fail. The engine room began to sink into complete silence. Her hand began to shake even more. When she felt that a deathly chill had touched her body, she heard Mesthiri sing: '*Thaazhum thalirum mizhi pootti . . . thaze syamaamambarathin nizhallaayi . . .*' He kept repeating the thematic line of the song. After a few repetitions, Padmini turned slowly to him and in a shaky voice, corrected him. 'It is not *thaazum, thalirum.*'

Mesthiri stopped singing and looked at her.

'Really? Then what is it?'

Managing to collect words on her shrivelled lips, she said: 'It is . . . *thaarum thalirum . . .*'

Mesthiri was quiet for a few moments and then he told her: 'Ok, then. Sing the song correctly now.'

Padmini nodded and asked for some water.

Pappan brought her some water. She drank it all in a single gulp and wiped her lips with her left elbow.

Before she began to sing, Mesthiri gestured to Vava. He took the sword-stick from her.

Padmini began to sing the song. Mesthiri closed his eyes. She alone noticed that his eyes were welling.

Originally published as 'Vettu Road' in 2020

Scan QR code to access the
Penguin Random House India website